When the Flag Flies Again

By
Pauline K Murfin

1

Bobby Lennox, a romance writer, and her two best friends Suze and Penny, thought all their financial worries were a thing of the past when Bobby inherited Hollybush Station house, which could provide a home and a business venture for the girls.

Meanwhile, Major Alexander Balfour returns home from Iraq a broken man, destroyed was his lifelong dream of serving his country in the colours of the Royal Highland Regiment, The Black Watch.

After being invalided out of the army, in his attempt to heal himself physically and mentally from the horrors of his tour at Camp Dogwood, Alexander embarks on his father's dream; to restore and inhabit their ancestral home, Balfour Castle. But would the Balfour Flag ever fly again?

Pauline Murfin is a sixty two year old mother, with three grown up sons. Married for forty three years to husband Graham, they live in a remote village in Northumberland. Pauline and her husband Graham moved to a small village which is part of the Kielder Forest in the Northumberland National Park in 1999. Poor health prevented Pauline from working, so she decided to study for a degree with The Open University. "To keep my brain ticking over", after completing her degree and gaining a Bachelor of Science she turns her hand to writing fiction.

"Something I have always wanted to do" says Pauline.

Also by Pauline K Murfin

To Begin Again
Comraich
Dreams Lost Dreams Found
The Silent Connection
The Dainty Decorator

This book is dedicated to the usual suspects. To the best proof readers a person could have. Thank you, Elizabeth and Blanche for your continuous diligence in trawling through my raw manuscript in order that I don't make the most enormous gaffs.

To Pat and Val who enjoy my stories, which inspires me to carry on writing.

To Graham who continues to be my technical wiz of a husband, without his help I would not be the proud author of my sixth book.

To Rebecca Renieri for the wonderful cover design.

And finally to my new Copy Editor Sarah Foster, thank you Sarah for your very sympathetic interpretation of my manuscript. I hope this is the first of much collaboration together.

Chapter 1

"Oh my God, I must be mad," thought Roberta Lennox or Bobby, as she was known to her friends, scolding herself for abandoning her recently inherited home in the small village of Hollybush, only to steal away like a thief in the night in order to rent a broken down old shack in the middle of nowhere.

To be fair, the advert did say 'fisherman's cottage' on the beach for rent and that, it would appear, was exactly what it was. In fact it was so much a part of the dunes that if there was a sudden windstorm the shack was in danger of being swallowed completely, never to be found again.

"Well for goodness sake, let's at least give it a chance before condemning it out of hand," Bobby said aloud to herself. Yes it looked a little rickety and to actually get in to what looked like the only entrance, she would have to dig the sand away that had begun to build up against the little wooden weather-beaten door. But she decided that she wouldn't judge a book by its cover, and with that she began to look for the key that had apparently been left on the ledge above the little door; according to the reply she had received with her receipt for one month's rent. Only now did she wonder whether this sudden flush of having enough money to eat for a change was making her a little reckless with her meagre inheritance. Finding the large heavy metal key which looked more fitting to a castle keep than a tiny little shack, Bobby gingerly pushed it into the gaping mouth of a lock and gave it a firm turn.

The door creaked open and the heap of sand that had been leaning against the door entered before she did. It was still light enough to make out the interior of the little shack. Bobby's first impression as she peered into the semi darkness was that of the fading light of the evening peering inside like pink and gold fingers of light, stretching over the horizon before sinking beyond the skyline and into the ocean. All of this could be seen through the vast window at the front of the shack. A person would have to be blind not to see the sheer beauty of the white crests of rolling waves as they gradually came to rest on the shoreline.

"Well as long as there is a place to lay my sleepy head, charge my laptop and go to the loo, it couldn't be more perfect than this," Bobby decided there and then. And with a view like that; what more inspiration did a writer need for goodness sake. With a renewed determination she began to scan the shack for some sort of light before she lost the daylight altogether.

After almost whacking herself in the face, Bobby stumbled upon an old storm lamp hanging on a heavy metal hook from the ceiling just above the window. On the table set into the shallow bay of the window was a handy box of matches. After pumping and pulling levers in the hope that this would release or pump some sort of fuel distribution Bobby lit a match and held it against the frail looking mantle. Then with a gentle 'pop' the fragile-looking mantle jumped to life and then settle down to a bright glow.

Bobby wasn't exactly sure how she had done it but it would seem she had lit the lantern and to be honest it appeared to be brighter than most electric lights; if you discounted the fact that it sort of hissed, it was a very pleasant warming light.

The light was easily bright enough to allow good scrutiny of the little shack, which on closer inspection, wasn't so little after all. In fact it was rather like a tardis. The inside looked far roomier than it could possibly be, judging by the outside. It had a rather sturdy-looking stone fireplace with an ancient-looking log burner inset. A good supply of logs were piled high in the inglenook of the fireplace so they should be nice and dry, thought Bobby.

Two old armchairs were strategically placed for comfort and warmth, thought Bobby, and a very elderly sofa. The kind you saw in posh houses that you know must have cost a fortune and had seen many a good day; in normal homes it would have been relegated to the dump. However, it was perfectly useable and served its purpose; for the comfort of fisherman who wouldn't care that the material was faded beyond recognition.

Next to the large window a little table sat comfortably inside the space. The perfect place to write and gain inspiration from the different moods of the sea, thought Bobby fancifully. "This," she told herself out loud, "was what was meant by suffering for one's art." A small laugh escaped her fanciful thoughts before she moved on through into what was obviously the kitchen; small, well, miniscule, would have been a better description. However she simply needed to have a way of heating cans of soup or frying the odd fish, which she hoped would be good enough to jump out of the sea obligingly.

Bobby was slightly more concerned about the ablution facilities, and as she gingerly pushed open the last sturdy wooden door she was pleasantly surprised. Actually the small but adequate room had obviously had a recent coat of cream emulsion paint. There was the obligatory loo and a shower cubicle in the corner of the room and there was even a small radiator, although it certainly wouldn't throw out much heat it would be enough to take the chill off. However, common sense told Bobby that the power, water and loo were not simply as they were in your normal household and there must some instructions which she needed to find pretty quickly, especially the toilet instructions.

"Ah ha!" exclaimed Bobby as she spied an exercise book hanging by a piece of string from a hook in the kitchen. Where else would the instructions be for the electric than beside the small three ring cooker. A quick scan of the book soon told her that there was a septic tank system for the toilet, a generator for power to the lights, cooker and shower etc. There was also a fresh water delivery every three months to a mains tank that could be found to the back of the cottage.

Bobby decided she would think of it as a cottage from now on as it was not half as primitive as she had first thought. In actual fact it was a very sturdily built stone cottage though the roof looked as though parts of it had been replaced many times over the years. Bobby presumed it must blow off in high winds, although as the cottage had bedded itself into the sand dune she was surprised the wind would affect it at all. No, all in all Bobby decided it wasn't such a shack after all.

She brought her bags in from the car, which mostly consisted of carrier bags of food. She hadn't bothered bringing many clothes along, as her intention was to become a hermit and simply write. Once she had brought everything in from her battered old Citroen 2cv [which was probably the only kind of car apart from a four wheel drive which would be able to navigate over the humps and bumps of the dunes and not sink], Bobby thought she had better try to make some sense of the instructions for the toilet and generator. As she turned the tap on in the kitchen sink it came as a huge relief when the water came spluttering out of the decrepit tap. Well at least that appeared to need no further instruction, other than if you use too much you will run out, presumably. For a girl who has been used to student digs following instructions was second nature. And luckily she had always been the practical one of the three who had all shared the old student house in Dumfries.

A generator, now that's something new thought Bobby, however, how hard could it be? She had after all, managed the lantern which was hissing away and she could see no problems with the necessary [loo]. Bobby took a few minutes to have a poke around the tiny cottage, peering out of the window and in the distance she caught a glimpse of a lone figure walking along the water's edge.

Walking didn't exactly describe his actions, thought Bobby. The man seemed to be doing a sort of forced march with his face leaning into the wind and every movement of his slight figure seemed to be pushing him forward. Bobby noticed he had a fairly pronounced limp yet this didn't seem to slow him down; in fact he marched doggedly forward. It was then that Bobby noticed the two dogs walking by his side; they were not your average dogs out for a run on the beach. They looked from a distance to be skinny mongrel-like dogs. But like the man, they did not waste time on the frivolities of the incoming tide or the odd piece of driftwood, perfect for picking up and running with in the hope that their master would throw it for them.

Bobby watched the strange looking threesome until they disappeared out of sight. It crossed her mind that the beach was privately owned so he must have had permission to be there. Although intrigued by the odd little group, Bobby resumed her settling in process. The bedroom was a plain affair with two single beds in it. Piled on the bottom of each bed was what appeared to be fresh linen that consisted of a single quilt, fresh quilt cover, bottom sheet and two pillowcases.

It was all very functional and clean, more than could be expected for fishermen, Bobby supposed. It was simple but perfect. After all, wasn't this what she had wanted? Peace and quiet. A place to write undisturbed by 'creepy Kevin'.

Chapter 2

It was certainly strange how when Bobby lived in the old student house in Dumfries with Penny and Suze, she could write without a problem, even with various boyfriends coming and going. Usually 'going,' as all three girls had decided that they must have incredibly high standards since they found their preferred qualities more and more difficult to find in the men they chose.

Bobby, Penny and Suze had met fresh faced and brimming with enthusiasm when they had all applied for a student house to share in Dumfries. Bobby, whose chosen degree was in Journalism, was quite tall at five foot seven and fairly slim with generous curves in all the right places and a shock of long wavy black hair. Penny, slim with long blonde hair and pale skin, intended to be an astute businesswoman when she graduated in Business and Marketing. Suze, the smallest of the three at only five foot four inches with what could be called a buxom or generous figure, aspired to be head chef and run her own restaurant.

The three girls took an instant liking to each other and chose to live together all through university. Then after graduation none of them felt the need to move on. Like a family they supported one another and when jobs were not forthcoming in their chosen profession it was Bobby's writing that saved the day. Well, it paid the rent and kept the lights on, at least!

Bobby always wanted to be a journalist as she loved to write however, from the very first assignment she handed in to her tutor it was obvious that Bobby did not have and never would have the cut-and-thrust qualities of a killer journalist. From the day Bobby started university she had a clear idea of her future and that she would be a journalist with a heart, someone who would show that sad stories could be reported without a heart of stone. She would be the outstanding female journalist who would win prizes for truth and justice that would be delivered with sympathy.

However, by the time Bobby graduated with a meagre 2.2 degree it was clear that she lacked the single-minded hunger for a real life drama where she should be indifferent and ruthless in the pursuit of a good story. Bobby could not take advice on how to report a story without her own opinions impinging on the truth. Hence the writing of the books came about where she had her tutor to thank for the income that kept all three girls from starving at times. Her tutor tried in vain to advise Bobby that she had to be more realistic and single-minded if she was to become a journalist in the real world. However, she told Bobby she had a friend who was a publisher of romantic novels and she felt sure that Bobby would be more suited to fiction than fact. Once the pair had been introduced the rest was history.

Bobby would always be grateful to her tutor as she found after a while that she had in fact, been right. She really could never have become the in-your-face type of journalist she would need to have been to further her career. Her writing meant a lot to her and Bobby knew one day she would not simply write romantic fiction, one day a subject would touch her so deeply that she would be compelled to write about it. But until that day she felt very lucky that she was able to stay at home and write and be paid; meanwhile Penny and Suze had to embark upon a variety of horrendous jobs in order to pay their share of the rent.

It was a particularly difficult month where Penny had been let go from the cheap and cheerful pound shop after a slump in profits forced the last in, first out policy of redundancy. And Suze had been in yet another battle with a well-known burger chain for decorating the food at the drive-in to "make it look more appetising," she claimed, was also asked to leave.

It was that morning when Bobby received a letter from Messrs Murfin and Sykes solicitors,

informing her she had inherited The
Old Station at Hollybush in East
Ayrshire, from an old aunt she
hardly remembered. Although she
did remember going on one of the
few trips out with her mother and
father before they went their
separate ways. She was very little,
and it was to a small village with a
lovely name she recalled, to visit an
elderly lady who lived in a station
house. As Bobby stood mid step,
reading the letter over again in case
she had misunderstood its contents,
the memory became clearer.

The letter informed her she had
inherited the station, house and
outbuildings etc etc and she was to
contact the office on the following
phone number. Bobby flopped

down on her rickety office chair
with such a force there was a
protesting noise from underneath
which threatened to give up the
ghost completely.

As if the words would become
clearer Bobby read it again
however, it still said she had to
contact a solicitor and she had in
fact inherited a 'station and house'.
Bobby suddenly let out such a yell
of delight just as the front door
slammed shut and a voice from the
passage hollered, "It's only me."

Suze dashed in through the door to
see what on earth the commotion
was as Bobby thrust the letter into
her hands saying, "Read, read,
you're never going to believe it,

read it and tell me if it's true or just a joke."

"Shut up then and let me read it for God's sake!"

Suze tried to read and Bobby kept interrupting, so Suze began again to read the letter out loud, repeating what Bobby had read and saying aloud but tentatively as though it couldn't possibly be true.

"You have inherited a station… and a house… and some other buildings?"

"I have haven't I? That is what it says isn't it?"
"Yes, it says you have inherited a station, house and some other

buildings... Yes it's definitely true, do you know someone who owns a station?"

"I did, well I never actually knew her; she was a relative of my mothers. We went once when I was little, I remember it being in a lovely little village and it was called Hollybush Station. But she had to be ancient by now; I can't believe she has only just died. But have I really inherited a station? There is no catch?"

"Well there doesn't seem to be a catch; you won't know until you ring the solicitor. Ring them, ring them now, go on. I'll make us a coffee and you sit down and ring.

"Oh my God, I can't believe it, just as we need a miracle, here it is…. Oh but I'm not going to count my chickens until they're hatched or whatever the saying is…"

"Shut up Bobby, and ring the solicitor for goodness sake!"

Bobby sat down with the phone; dialling the number gingerly she took a deep breath and tentatively asked to speak to either Mr Sykes or Mr Murfin. Bobby held the receiver with Suze hanging over her shoulder in order to try to overhear what was being said but all she had gathered from Bobby was, "Yes, Yes, erm yes, thank you," which was driving Suze mad with curiosity. Finally Bobby replaced the receiver in its cradle and said in a disbelieving voice:

"It's true, it's true, I have inherited Hollybush Station and all the outbuildings and rolling stock, whatever that is. The keys and paperwork are being held at the village bank and will be released upon my signature."

"Yes, Yes, Yes!" was shouted in unison, at the top of their voices. While jumping up and down, in the middle of the tiny living room, into the pandemonium walked Penny.

A story told by two women at once was bad enough but a story screamed at the top of two excited, out of breath voices was almost unintelligible.

"Enough, enough, one at a time. Please tell me what the hell is going on; have we won the lottery?"

"Almost, you will never believe it, never!"

"Well tell me… somebody tell me something before I strangle you both."

"I have inherited a station."

"She has inherited a station."

Bobby thrust the letter from the solicitor's office into Penny's face, telling her to read while all the time telling her exactly what its contents was. Suze was giving a running commentary on "Outbuildings, rolling stock, whatever that is and it's called Hollybush, isn't that lovely?"

After reading the letter with the difficulty of both of the other girls interrupting constantly, Penny digested the gist of the letter and confirmed with Bobby that she had actually rang the solicitor's to be sure it wasn't some kind of cruel joke. Bobby replied that she had indeed spoken to a Mr Murfin who had confirmed she had inherited a station, et cetera. "And I have to collect the key and paperwork and such at the village bank."

Chapter 3

Had all that been just one year ago?
Bobby thought back to the day
when all three girls had piled into
her old Citroen 2cv and excitedly
began the journey from Dumfries to
Hollybush. When they arrived in
the village less than two hours later,
it was hard to imagine that such an
enchanting little village was
literally only fifty miles away from
Dumfries. Yet it was a world away
from the dull red stone houses and
drab streets that they had become
accustomed to since beginning their
student life several years ago.

 Bobby drove slowly through the
village looking for the bank, where
she must report to in order to collect

the keys for the old station. The excited "Ooh's" and "Ahh's" from the other two girls were becoming contagious and Bobby's tummy began to make funny squirming feelings at the realisation that in a very few minutes she would be the official owner of her very own station.

"Oh look, an Antique shop and a pub no two pubs, oh that looks like a nice pub. A newspaper shop, handy, and oh look a home bakers, oh wow, when was the last time you had home baking?" Chimed both girls excitedly in Bobby's ears, as she drove steadily through the village in search of the bank.

"Oh, there's the bank on the corner. Wow I'm surprised it still has a bank in such a small village. Park here, Bobby."

"Yes I know, what are you both like, I do the driving and you get to see all the sights. It is sweet though isn't it? I can almost, remember it. Well here goes, girls."

As they parked the ancient car outside the bank all three girls linked arms saying "One for all and all for one," as they had often quoted when only one of them was earning and they all had to share. They walked purposefully, seemingly back in time, into the very old bank. It reminded you of the kind of bank you went in with your mother as a child, the smell of the wood and the polished floors, reminiscent of a bygone era.

As the girls pushed Bobby towards the old fashioned counter, the little old lady with the horn-rimmed spectacles peered down her nose at the trio, she also appeared to be from a bygone era. In fact the whole set up was rather surreal; it was as though they were in a time warp. Suddenly, as though from out of nowhere, there appeared a youngish man, who towered over the little biddy with the horn-rimmed specs.

"I'll take it from here Miss Frith thank you, I've been expecting the young lady."

This was said in an enquiring manner, as to which of the young ladies was Miss Roberta Lennox. He was a man in his forties thought Bobby, quiet refreshingly less stuffy than the actual ambience of the bank. However there was something a little unsettling about him, thought Bobby which could possibly be his smile, it seemed a little too gushing for a first time meeting.

However, thought Bobby, this was probably all in her imagination and he was probably a really nice guy. He looked roughly in his forties and wasn't unattractive in a bland sort of way. His clothes didn't help much he almost blended into his tan coloured suit with a fawn shirt and equally bland coloured tie. This Bobby supposed, was a step up from the pinstripe suits bank managers used to wear, so maybe he was a little more modern than the bank itself.

Bobby introduced herself and held out her hand to shake his hand as he replied, "My name is Kevin Hamilton, I am the branch manager."

Bobby shook his hand and hoped it was her imagination that he seemed to hold onto her hand just that little bit longer than was necessary, making one feel a little uncomfortable.

"Shall we go through to my office?"

There he went again thought Bobby, with that overly enthusiastic grin. The girls all trooped through into his office. It was very in keeping with the rest of the bank's décor, which Bobby thought was probably early 1920s.

"Please ladies, have a seat and let's get down to the business in hand shall we, that is unless you would prefer to speak privately about your inheritance Miss Lennox. Your friends could wait in the outer office, I'm sure Miss Frith could find them a cup of tea?"

"Oh no, my friends are with me and anything you have to tell me can certainly be said in front of them as we have no secrets."

"Oh, that's very commendable I must say," replied Kevin in such a way that indicated he really didn't agree however, as the client had requested it he had little choice.

"Well at present it's simply a matter of handing over the keys to the station, house, and outbuildings and a letter of explanation on the cash settlement which your aunt left you. I'm sure you would like to see the property first and digest the letter at your leisure, so I propose that you first take your time in looking over the old station and if you have any queries come back and see me again. You would be most welcome Miss Lennox."

"Oh it's Bobby please and that sounds a great idea. It's a very, very long time since I visited the old station and I'm very anxious to see it again. I will certainly come back if I have any problems, and thank you so much for your personal attention; I'm sure you're a very busy man."

Bobby would soon learn to regret those few words 'personal attention' in the course of time.

Chapter 4

After full instructions on how to find the station and collecting the bulky envelope, which held numerous heavy keys, they all shook hands and off they went excitedly back to Bobby's battered old car. Excited though she was, Bobby couldn't shake off a foreboding feeling yet she couldn't for the life of her think why. I mean for goodness sake, how often do you ever inherit anything, let alone a station and she had the keys in her hot little hand so there was no mistake. What on earth could there be to worry about?

They found the station yard very easily; in fact it was just off the main village street. It was very handy for the pub they all thought and the shops; the typical student mentality was difficult to shake. As they climbed out of the car, all three girls stood speechless before blurting out, "Oh my God, you have inherited a station... and a *train!* For goodness sake, that must be what they meant by rolling stock! And how many outbuildings are there for goodness sake? "

As the three girls ran almost like children from building to building, becoming more and more excited as they found nooks and crannies within each of the buildings, they suddenly stopped and gave out the most enormous scream!

"You've inherited *a station and a train!* Bloody hell Bobby; what are you going to do with it all?"

"Well the house is lovely and it only needs a little updating, it's quaint the way it is so I wouldn't want to change anything."

"No I meant, are you going to sell it? Or what?" Asked Penny.
"Oh no Bobby, don't sell," Demanded Suze. All three girls turned and looked towards the enormous train, just standing motionless by what had once been the platform, before breaking into a run to explore excitedly. The train was actually in amazingly good condition, it was as though it had simply pulled into the station and

just never left again. The outside was maroon and cream and the inside had bright blue platform bench seats with a table between each cubicle.

They almost ran through the train like children on a day out, with Bobby shouting, "You're not going to believe this, there is a loo here."

"It feels almost like a runaway train with only us as travellers."
Said Penny.

Suze was looking very seriously at the front end of the train, and she had a look on her face that said she had an idea. As they all came to rest in on the bench seats Suze said in a tentative and slight disbelieving way, "Do you know Bobby, this would make a great tea room, can you see it? You could have the little kitchen at the front and all the booths have ready-made tables…. Can you just imagine it, there wouldn't be that much work to do either, simply get an electrician to work out the logistics of the cooking facilities… what do you think, do you see it?"

"Oh Suze, that's a wonderful idea," Said Bobby, "Although I wouldn't want to have anything to do with it. It would be your venture, all yours. Could you do it?"

"Oh Bobby I would give my right arm to run my own little place, it would be a dream come true!"

As Suze began to almost cook and serve in her head, Penny jumped in.

"Bobby, what would you think about me having the waiting room as a gift shop, I noticed as we came through the village they didn't appear to have one? Oh God Bobby, I would give my right eye if I could start a business as well?"

"Well, Suze with your right arm, Penny's right eye, and me becoming a famous author in my own little station house, we can't fail. All for one and one for all!"

Both Suze and Penny were now insisting that it all be on a business footing and they pay their way.

They promised in unison that Bobby should get a fair rent and a percentage of the profits. All the girls excitedly babbled about how they all wanted to be fair and that they would never take advantage of Bobby.

They decided all that talk about food and tearooms that they were suddenly hungry and Suze remembered one of the pubs had a sign outside saying takeaway food. They nipped up the main street and bought a selection of takeaways and a couple of bottles of wine to celebrate. As they drifted towards the old train and sat at the ready-made tables to eat their supper and excitedly make plans for the future, Suze smiled a satisfied smile.

"Did you notice how we automatically came to the train to eat? It's the perfect, perfect place for a tearoom. Oh I can't wait, I will call it the… Train… erm the … no the coaches… No, no – the Carriages, YES! The Carriages. Oh I can't wait!"

Penny was excitedly deciding what kind of stock she would have, how she would lay out the gift shop and how she thought visitors would come and spend their cash in the shop, then have a coffee at Suze's tea rooms; it was all going to be perfect.
Then suddenly reality hit and both girls realised that they were going to need money to be able to do the

changes they needed, even for paint, fittings and electricians et cetera. A sudden attack of reality hit the happy band with a thump, until Bobby broke the silence saying,

"Hang on let's think this through, didn't Mr Hamilton say there was a cash settlement? Well we don't know yet how much cash there is going to be." Both girls jumped in saying that they couldn't take advantage of Bobby like that and they would have to think of another way. Until Penny who always did have a head for finance, offered a suggestion that she told Bobby she could say no to if she didn't agree and she would totally understand – but before she could introduce her plan Bobby jumped in.

"Listen, we're totally forgetting the buildings are all paid for aren't they? So isn't there a way that I could borrow from them? You know a kind of business loan? Penny you know more about it than me, what do you think?"

"Well actually I had the same thought as you. Then, it means if we took an official loan from you, we could then have a proper repayment plan for when the businesses begin to make a profit. I would feel much more comfortable making things official Bobby, I know you will argue but I won't have it any other way and I'm sure Suze will feel the same as me so we'll have no argument about it."

"I totally agree with Penny," added Suze. "In fact it's better this way because then we will feel as though they are our businesses and we are not simply sponging off you. I for one can't wait to be my own boss and earn money for me for a change, instead of some faceless organisation with no 'flair'."

"Well then it's agreed. We'll go back to the bank in the morning and I'll have a word with Mr Hamilton and find out how to go about taking a loan. The three girls planned and plotted how, when and what needed doing and roughly how much they thought things would cost. They also made a list of tradesmen they would need to give them quotes.

The excitement was palpable and all three girls could not have been happier. This was a dream come true for all of them.

Chapter 5

Bobby sat curled up with her knees
tucked beneath her in one of the
very comfortable old armchairs by
the glowing log burner, which had
been surprisingly easy to light. In
the fading light of the evening she
saw the silhouette of the unknown
person and his dogs. He was not
quite marching now, his shoulders
were more hunched and his face fell
lower He didn't slow his pace
though and neither did his dogs. As
he disappeared into the distance
Bobby became even more curious.
Who was this man who seemed to
push himself to the limit and his
loyal followers who never strayed
from his side?

As the warmth from the log burner touched Bobby's face and she sunk lower into the comfy armchair her thoughts returned to her reason for her grand escape. Was it an escape or simply a retreat to extricate her from a situation she had begun to find suffocating? She hadn't wanted to hurt Kevin's feelings; but he had inveigled himself into her life. On reflection Kevin had inserted himself into Bobby's life rather like that creeping plant, oh what was it? thought Bobby, the one that grew in the garden of the old student digs. Morning Glory! Its flower was rather pretty when you first saw it, then before you knew it; it grew and grew and grew until it suffocated everything else in the garden.

Kevin had been like that. The morning after all three girls had made their plans for the future it was agreed that Bobby would go alone to the bank and see Mr Hamilton or Kevin as he would insist she call him on that meeting. He told Bobby that she had also inherited five thousand pounds in cash. This news he delivered as though he personally was giving it to Bobby. When Bobby explained the girls' plans to him he was very sceptical about her generosity towards her two friends. Bobby explained that it was her wish and not only that, she trusted her two friends like the sisters she felt they had become.

Seeing he would never change Bobby's mind, Kevin agreed to the loan and he would draw up the loan documents for all the girls to sign. Little did Bobby know that this was to be the beginning of the slow drip, drip, drip of Kevin's involvement into her life.

Being students for so long, then earning and managing their own lives since graduating, the girls were very independent of outsiders. Their motto of 'all for one and one for all' had seen each of them through some lean times, so this miracle was their eureka moment, the start they had all been waiting for.

From the outset Kevin seemed not to trust Suze and Penny and made an obvious beeline for Bobby, as if to protect her interests. It never dawned on Bobby that he seemed to take an inordinate amount of interest in their small loans. He insisted on making up separate business plans and assessments for both Suze and Penny's individual loans. He would constantly make suggestions as to how Bobby should recoup her money. Bobby didn't mention his suggestions to the girls as it was of no importance to her whether they ever paid her back. They would pay her a rent that would cover the cost of the loan, when they were established. If and when they became very successful then they would discuss it again.

What began as constant interference about Suze and Penny then began to intrude on Bobby's life. Kevin had insisted he needed Bobby's mobile number in case he needed to contact her on a matter of business however, in reality it was simply another way of constantly texting and ringing about trivial matters.

Bobby should have been blissfully happy in her cosy station cottage; she should have been able to write without the constant interruptions which used to occur when they all shared a lounge at the old digs. Suze and Penny were so busy she hardly saw them until late in the evening when they would grab a bite to eat together before both girls fell into bed exhausted but happy at the progress of their burgeoning businesses. Bobby got less writing done than she ever had before. She felt unsettled at the constant invasion of her private space, by Kevin's constant unexpected visits. Occasionally all three girls would spontaneously decide to go to the pub and have a drink like old times only to find Kevin would arrive as though by radar.

Suze and Penny thought it was rather sweet that he appeared to have a crush on Bobby; they would not have found him quite so sweet if they knew about his constant badgering to Bobby about the terms and conditions of their loan agreements. When Bobby refused to take any rent from the girls until they were settled and making a profit, Kevin could be quite forceful as though it were up to him to protect Bobby's investment.

Bobby had to gently but firmly explain on one particular occasion when Kevin was becoming obsessive, that after all it was her mortgage and her profit or loss and as long as the payments were being paid to the bank, which they were from the income from her books plus a little from her small capital, then there was no need for the bank's intervention. Kevin had not liked Bobby's rebuke, telling her in his hurt and pouting fashion that he only meant if for the best and was simply looking out for her.

Then there was the occasion, thought Bobby, in her reminiscences of why she had finally decided to disappear for a while. The occasion when Kevin had cornered her on one of his unannounced visits to her cottage, on his previous attempts to kiss her, Bobby managed to evade being kissed on the mouth and the stray kiss landed on her unyielding cheek. However on this occasion Kevin seemed to have planned his strategy and taken Bobby by surprise as she turned towards the sound behind her while working, Kevin took this opportunity to plant a warm wet kiss on Bobby's surprised, slightly parted lips.

So pleased was he with his success he grabbed hold of Bobby's arms and pulled her out of her seat and into his arms. It took Bobby a minute to get over the sheer audacity and shock of being yanked out of her chair while in the depths of typing her current novel. She pulled back against Kevin's arms while attempting to keep a smile on her face so as not to alert him to what would happen next if he didn't let go. Bobby, Suze and Penny had not been students with amorous suitors without learning exactly where to knee a man when and if the need arose.

Luckily for Kevin he released her just in time and was unaware of how close he had come to physical injury. However, that had been the moment when Bobby decided she needed to get away.

She knew the girls would be fine as they were so busy they would hardly miss her. She would let them know where and why she had to disappear for a while when she got to wherever she was going. It was then that Bobby remembered she had seen an ad while browsing the local paper; it was for a fisherman's cottage that was for rent. Bobby hunted for the paper and quickly leafed through it. Finding the ad she read that it was on the beach and had all the facilities she could require. The cottage was on the Ayrshire coast near Lungar, Craobh Haven. The words sounded sweet to Bobby who decided there and then to pack a few things.

It had been an awkward moment getting Kevin to leave after his amorous pass, however he sensed that he had better give Bobby a chance to adjust to the change in their burgeoning relationship, or so he thought.

Chapter 6

The rest, as they say, is history. Setting off from her cottage Bobby left her phone behind so that she could not be contacted. She dashed a quick note for each of the girls, leaving Suze's on the train and Penny's through the letter box of the gift shop; that way there would be no way for Kevin to see them. She bought enough food to last a couple of weeks at the local supermarket where she also purchased a cheap pay-as-you-go mobile with which she would use for emergencies only and to contact the girls when she was settled. Clothes were not a problem, as she had no intentions of socialising. Hopefully.

After having an amazingly good night's sleep, in which Bobby felt remarkably safe considering she was alone in a cottage on an empty beach. Bobby almost leaping out of bed made the instant decision that she couldn't wait to have a brisk walk along the private beach. This she thought to herself, would surely give her an appetite, something she had lacked for the last few months. The cottage it would seem, got some form of sunshine all day long as she remembered the last rays streaming in last night and the little lounge was bathed in the warmth of the early summer sun this morning, lifting her recently dull mood to a feeling of pure exhilaration.

It was early May and the sun was not at its full height, so Bobby pulled her old college hoody and a pair of denims from the stack of clothes which lay on the spare bed. "Comfort, yes comfort that's definitely going to be the order of this break, comfort and simple pleasures, and some productive writing," Bobby said out loud as if to make it a hard and fast rule to be adhered to. There was a slight breeze but as the beach seemed to drop below the dunes it felt protected and really quite warm. Bobby breathed in the fresh salty air and for the first time in over a year she actually felt free. She drifted along the beach until the little cottage was almost out of sight before she eventually turned around and began her slow amble back.

She suddenly realised that she felt as though she could eat a horse. This was a feeling she hadn't felt in a long time either, not since the girls would have a sudden flush of money and they would treat themselves to bacon, eggs and fresh soft bread with lashings of butter on a Sunday morning. This didn't happen often enough to worry about the amount of calories they had consumed in one meal.

But suddenly Bobby realised that in some ways she missed those days, the days when they had nothing more to worry about than whether or not they had enough money to feed the gas meter. She didn't wish that she hadn't inherited the station; of course that would be plain silly, and of course Suze and Penny couldn't be happier. They had both gone from strength to strength in their different business ventures. Suze's tearooms were an instant hit in the village and the gift shop was just what visitors had wanted and the fact that they were both within tottering distance of each other made it all the better.

It was simply that apart from creepy Kevin making her life a pain, she didn't feel as though she had achieved anything unlike the others. She knew that she could kick creepy Kevin in to touch, if she really had to. He did hold sway with the bank however, and could make things difficult for her, although if she had become really worried and uncomfortable she would have told the others and they would have sorted Kevin out despite his hold over their loans, she knew that without a doubt. No, it was more than that; she was becoming more and more unsatisfied with the books she wrote, and yes they had been good to her and the girls. Perhaps she had begun to feel as though her work was rather trivial. Was she a little jealous of the others' success? No, no, surely not? Well not their success, definitely not, but their advances into new territory maybe. The excitement they were feeling at their new ventures yes… Yes she supposed that was part of her problem. She was a little disappointed in herself for settling, she had settled for the easy way out. At first writing romances had been the temporary stopgap, a way of paying the bills. It was always meant to be temporary until she wrote her 'magnum opus'. As Bobby drifted back towards the little cottage in the warm sunshine she wondered what had become of her dream of writing something worthwhile, something deep and meaningful? She had simply forgotten about it.

Well, thought Bobby with renewed vigour, I have remembered now! And I promise myself here and now that I, Roberta Lennox, will do myself justice and write something that comes from deep within my heart and soul, before I return to the outside world. And with that rousing thought, Bobby reached the cabin with a hunger that was as new to her as her newly acquired ambition.

After having a hearty breakfast of poached eggs on toast and two huge mugs of coffee, Bobby set her lap top up on the table after having the generator going for the last two hours she imagined she would have enough charge left in her lap top to do at least two or three chapters of her current book. She was at the last stage, the part where all the pieces fitted together like a jigsaw puzzle and the two lovers would of course find each other and walk off into the sunset. She had written this a hundred times and knew she would accomplish this in less than a week.

There really couldn't be a better time than this if Bobby was serious about her intention to write something of note. The first thing she must do if she was serious was to get in touch with the owner of the cabin and ask if she could extend her rental, but for how long? Bobby began thinking how long she could afford to pay without earning an income. She decided that she would extend her lease to the end of July, supposing that the cottage was free. She found the receipt which the owner had sent which luckily had the phone number on it. Deciding there was no time like the present she dialled the number and a deep voice came straight to the point, barking out, "Balfour."

"Oh err hi, my name is Bobby Lennox and I am at present staying in your cottage on the beach and I wondered if the cottage was booked for the two months following my lease?"

There was an inordinately long silence, so much so that Bobby began to repeat her message in case the man at the other end hadn't heard her the first time.

"You are Bobby Lennox? And you are a… woman?"

"Yes I am most certainly a woman, although I don't quite follow you."

"You hired the cottage for the month of May and you are a woman? Are you with your boyfriend or husband?

"Yes…" answered Bobby, feeling as though she were in the middle of some sort of comedy sketch, "I am a woman and no, I am not with a boyfriend and I don't have a husband."

"Do you fish?"

"Fish? No, I don't fish, I'm afraid I don't understand, I am a writer"

"Ah, I see, so you hired the cottage to write?"

"Yesss…." Bobby said patiently as though the man might be a little slow, "And I would like to know if it is available until the end of July?"

"Erm, yes the cottage is available," was the reply, "But are you sure the cottage is what you want?" The voice said in a slightly less aggressive tone. "I'm sure there are other places far better suited to your needs, Miss Lennox?"

"No I'm fine," reassured Bobby, "The cottage is exactly what I need, I simply need the basics and it's certainly basic but adequate. I wondered if you could take my card number, as I haven't brought a chequebook with me. I could always go to a cash machine over the next few days but I just wanted to be sure that you hadn't booked up for those months."

"No it isn't booked and don't worry about the money, when you next go to the cash machine will be fine as you are already paid up for the month anyway. But are you sure it has the amenities you require, I mean after all it's only meant for fishermen, therefore it is rather rough and ready."

His voice had softened a little after his initial brisk manner; his initial thought was maybe that she had called to complain about the cottage.

"This may seem a silly question but would you like me to send you the money or…."

"No, no I can collect it one day, I usually walk along the beach a couple of times a day with the dogs, so I can just call if that suits you?"

"Oh yes, er that'll be fine by me, I'll be here, er thank you very much er.. Mr …Balfour?"

Bobby heard a distant thank you as though on afterthought he remembered before replacing his receiver. Ah! So he is the mystery dog man, well that answers how he has permission to be on a private beach.

Bobby was on a mission for the rest of the week; she worked like a demon and without any interruptions she even amazed herself when she finally typed 'The End', on her happy ever after romantic fiction. Her heart felt lighter not just because the guy got the girl, but because she had worked with the sole purpose of completing this book knowing she was going to write something new, something with meaning She felt slightly exhilarated at the thought of not just knocking out yet another work of fiction.

She was also, when she stopped to think about the task ahead, rather nervous. It had been a long time since Bobby had left her comfort zone. In fact not since she had been at university and doing her degree had she wrote anything meaningful.

"First thing's first Roberta," she stated aloud, "I better check in with HQ [the girls], I'll send this off to the publishers, [her usb stick with her book safely recorded on it] and then I better draw some cash in case the mysterious walker calls."

Bobby drove her little old car out of the sand dune, amazed at how it crawled gradually but steadily out of the little hole it had dug itself into over the last couple of weeks. She knew she had better get in more food supplies as she didn't intend to do this run very often and the nearest decent supermarket was quite a distance away.

As she drove up from the beach and along a short road to towards a fairly busy B road leading towards the town, she passed the gatehouse of what she presumed to be the old castle. She had seen a turret from the beach, and assumed that the old castle was derelict. She presumed in that case that the man on the phone must live in the gatehouse.

Her purchases stashed inside the beat up old car and having drawn enough cash to pay for the further two months Bobby decided on a takeaway coffee which she would drink in the car and at the same time ring each of the girls. She would keep it simple and just say she intended to spend a few months writing and not to worry about her. With some trepidation she dialled Suze's mobile number only to be greeted with some sort of tornado.

"Where the hell are you? We have been frantic.. My God if that 'creep' has been bothering you, you should have told us and we'd have blacked his eyes. For God's sake Bobby, you should have told us."

This was Suze in her agitated state, where she would fight with a feather for her friends. "Wait there, I'll just get the little girl from the village, she helps me to serve now." Within seconds Suze was back and

sparks were flying in defence of
Bobby once again.

"Will you listen to me…please
Suze! I shouldn't have worried you,
telling you that Kevin was
becoming overly amorous and more
touchy feely. But hey listen will
you stop worrying, it was nothing I
couldn't handle. I promise I would
have brought in the big guns if he
had become too persistent. But to
be honest Suze I wasn't getting any
work done, his constant pestering
was really getting on my ………
you know?"

"You should have told us Bobby,
you should have said and we
wouldn't have thought it was just a
crush. Listen, where the hell are you

anyway? You didn't say in your note."

"Well I'm coming to that. I've rented a cottage on the beach and it's wonderful, it's very basic but I'm working. I've finished my book, and now…. Well now I'm going to write something for me, I want to write something more important than just romantic fiction. Do you know what I mean? Don't get me wrong, I'm not jealous of you and Penny, but I feel I'm wasting my time and I'm not producing anything. I haven't fulfilled my dream like you and Penny have. I know you'll understand. I've rented the cottage until the end of July and I'll give you my mobile number, my new one so that only you and Penny can reach me. I left my other one behind because Kevin must have had me in his bloody speed dial. Do you know sometimes he would text me up to ten times a day for absolutely nothing? I simply couldn't think. Actually Suze, he's done me the power of good as I was about to become very comfortable in my own little cottage knocking out romantic fiction and forgetting that I once had ambition, just as you and Penny had, but you've achieved your goal. Well, it's what I hope to do, I don't know what the hell I'm going to write about or even if I can, but I'm going to give it a damned good go. So please don't worry about me and listen will you tell Penny, explain it all so I have

don't have to have another ear
bashing from her?"

"Yes, yes anything you say, but
Bobby you don't have to prove
anything to anyone. You are a
writer; we know that more than
anyone. How do you think we have
all lived for the last four or five
years for goodness sake, but I know
what you mean and we'll support
you. Please don't stay away because
of creepy Kevin for goodness sake
though, because we would sort him
out… oh you are not going to
believe this! You'll enjoy this, his
uncle has a business in the village
and you'll never guess what it is….
Hamilton's the Undertakers.!!! Ha
ha ha, no wonder Kevin is so
creepy, it must run in the family."

"How is business anyway, enough about me?"

"Oh Bobby it's brilliant, it couldn't be better I've even employed a young girl from the village to help out. I can't bake fast enough, and apparently everyone in the village thinks it's the best place ever and they wonder what they did before we arrived. Penny is selling the most gorgeous stuff and to be honest I can't go in without wanting to buy something myself. There is talk about the bus that comes through the village once an hour being diverted to the station as a sort of terminus which would mean even more customers, can you believe it? Oh but listen to me babbling on. Are you sure you are OK Bobby really, really, Penny will kill me if she thinks you rang and were in trouble and all I could do was talk about was The Carriages and The Gift Shop."

"I am fine, never been happier and I'm full of renewed enthusiasm. Don't beat yourself up about telling me how great things are going, wasn't that always our dream? All for one and one for all. Well bye for now and don't forget you can always ring me but don't–"

"I know, don't let creepy Kevin know where you are, never, never! Bye Bobby, I'll let Penny know that all is well."

Chapter 7

Still smiling after her encounter on the phone with Suze, her ferocious protector, , Bobby felt happier than she had a right to. She was embarking on an unknown project, far away from her friends and comfort zone, yet it felt right. That's not to say she didn't have more than her fair share of nerves at this moment in time, but they were the kind that you got when you had revised for an exam and knew you should do well but were still little unsure.

By the time Bobby got back to the cottage it was late afternoon. She stowed all her shopping in the cottage and made herself a quick

sandwich, which she decided she
would eat 'alfresco'. She collected
her small notepad and pen and
wandered towards the water's edge.
The sun was still high in the sky but
there was not a lot of heat in it as it
was still early in the year. In fact, it
was decidedly comfortable, the
breeze warming her face.

Whilst finishing her sandwich
Bobby came upon the remains of a
large tree which was no more than
driftwood now and she wished she
had artistic tendencies as she felt
sure an artist would make
something really 'arty and cool' out
of it. As she sat down on the tree,
pen in hand and book at the ready,
letting her eyes wander along the
deserted little beach, it began to

dawn on Bobby that her inspiration was going to have to come from within as there was nothing of any significance on the horizon or likely to be in the near future.

"Don't push it, it'll come," Bobby told herself firmly and as she wandered along the water's edge, something made her lift her eyes to the far end of the beach and instantly she knew it was her mystery marcher whom she now thought was Mr Balfour. Well who else could it be? As he got closer and closer with his two loyal dogs running by his side, it was clear to Bobby that they were going to have to pass the time of day or it would look ridiculous. She wondered if either he or his dogs were quite as ferocious as he sounded on the phone. Well, she was going to find out soon enough.

Bobby made a gesture towards the two skinny mongrels as she had correctly guessed they were.

"Hello, hello…" Bobby began tentatively holding out her hand, to the far from aggressive dogs, in fact they appeared to be very, very nervous. They looked to their master who stopped his forced march to reassure the animals that she was not going to do them any harm.

As Bobby lifted her eyes momentarily from the dogs she was taken by surprise at the skeletally thin but muscular man with a taut expression on his face. Attempting not to stare, Bobby made a gesture towards the animals inviting the man to say if it was all right to touch them.

"Do they bite? I'm not scared of dogs but some people don't like you to touch their dogs."

"No, no they are fine just a little shell shocked and not used to a lot of strangers; you can pet them. In fact they are softies and love a bit of attention once they get used to you."

The stranger pointed to the very shy one, a really thin greyhound looking tan and white mongrel who almost cowered by his leg, telling Bobby that his name was Tariq and the other more inquisitive dog but of similar parentage was Nazim.

"Oh how lovely, what unusual names your dogs have." Bobby cooed over the animals and soon even Tariq was inquisitive enough to come closer to Bobby's hand that she held out towards them, allowing them to come to her rather than she pushes herself forward. Within a short space of time they had both sniffed her hand and appeared slightly less nervous. It was then that the deep voice she remembered from her phone conversation spoke.

"You must be the Bobby Lennox, whom I thought was a fisherman, but who in reality is a writer? My name is Alexander Balfour, Xander to my friends. The cottage belongs to the estate and I apologise again for its basic condition but as I mentioned on the phone it is actually just meant for fishermen who don't really care much about home comforts."

"Please don't apologise," protested Bobby. "Honestly, I have done more work in the last week than I have in a month at home; it's perfect for me really."

It was at that moment as Bobby glanced up from stroking the dogs she saw his face; she thought she saw a flicker in his taut muscled face. All she could think of was that this poor man needs feeding up! He looked thin and gaunt not unlike his dogs, yet Bobby could see he had beautiful features with the darkest eyes which for a very brief second before she looked away embarrassed, locked with hers.

He must have been roughly six foot two thought Bobby, her brain ticking away in a writer's fashion of taking in as many details in as many minutes. He had thick jet black hair plastered back after his forced march, his dark swarthy skin Bobby thought would tan readily. She couldn't help but notice he looked to be in some pain, or discomfort and very underweight. Bobby blurted out that she had been to the cash machine and could pay for another two months' rent anytime he wished to collect it.

By this time the reluctant animals were now close enough to sniff her jeans and their slim faces peered up at her as though looking to understand what she was saying.

"Don't worry about it, the cottage isn't always taken and I don't always advertise it, so it's not as though there are queues of fishermen wanting to rent it. You see, they have come around," Alexander said, pointing to his dogs.

"From now on they won't be afraid when they see you on the beach." It was his turn to snatch a glance at

Bobby. This time she felt his eyes on her in appraisal, not quite sure if she came out well or not. She blushed at the thought.

"If you find the solitude too much for you, feel free to have a wander up to the castle. I'm attempting to renovate it."

Bobby couldn't have been more surprised at the invitation from this seemingly brusque man. It just shows she thought to herself how wrong you can be about a person… and his dogs.

"I'd love to, thank you." she said to his fast retreating back as he began his forced march once again, his dogs immediately reattaching themselves to their master, and off into the distance the odd trio trekked.

Chapter 8

In the days that followed Bobby took to walking along the beach in the hope of some divine inspiration however, after three days she realised that this work of art was not simply going to hit her in an eureka moment, it was more likely to grow from normal day-to-day experiences. On the fourth day of battling with her lack of creativity Bobby could hear the faint noise of children's voices in the distance, she even heard the faint bark of a dog.

Aha, thought Bobby, natives! Intrigued to see who was invading her private little domain; she carried on walking towards the voices until they became quite audible. As she turned the little bend past one of the dunes she noticed the small group but the first thing she recognised was the two dogs. They were definitely Alexander Balfour's dogs. They were unmistakable without being cruel to their breed; they were distinctly mongrel.

Bobby carried on walking slowly so as to not frighten the small group who were probably not used to anyone else on the private beach. As she approached the two children, a boy and a girl, one of the dogs slowly made its way towards her, timidly but with purpose. Bobby held out her hand and spoke in a soft encouraging voice.

"Hello and which one are you?
Tariq or Nazim…?"

The dog recognising the tone of her
voice and obviously her scent and
came slowly forward to be stroked
very gently on the head.

"He almost never does that with
strangers does he, Mari?"

It was the boy of the group who had
spoken, who looked about seven or
eight thought Bobby, saying to the
little girl who looked slightly older.

"Well I met the dogs the other day
when your father was doing his
walk on the beach; and they must
have remembered my scent."
Bobby explained to the boy.

"Dad on the beach?" Said the little girl, with flame red hair, all waves tumbling down her back, in total contrast to the little boy who was as dark as Alexander.

"I doubt it would be Dad on the beach with Tariq and Nazim," explained the girl. They won't go with anyone except Uncle Xander as they are his dogs. They only come with us because we looked after them when they arrived and Uncle Xander was in hospital. He was injured in the war you know? Tariq and Nazim were his dogs. They shoot them you know, when the soldier is shipped home and Uncle Xander wouldn't let them, so he sent them home and we looked after them for him until he got well enough to come home."

Ah thought Bobby that answered a lot about the strange trio who marched the beach each day. About the stranger's looks, the skin that looked stretched over his face as though there wasn't a spare ounce of flesh on him, which there quite clearly wasn't. It answered the unasked question about the limp which he appeared to try so much to overcome and dismiss as though it wasn't there. And the dogs who looked like street urchins, the strays that roamed the streets abroad, attaching themselves to any kind face who was likely to feed them, leading to undying devotion.

"Ah you're right then it must have been your Uncle Xander I met. I'm Bobby by the way."

"You're the writer, Uncle Xander said he had rented you the shack, he's a bit embarrassed about that, he normally only rents it to fisherman as it's only the shack he and dad used to have sleepovers in when they were little. Hi, I'm Mari and this is Rory."

"Oh but I love it, and I don't mind at all that it's a bit basic but really I don't. So that was what the cottage was used for a long time ago."

The little boy laughed saying they never call it the cottage they always call it the shack on the beach.

"Yes Dad and Uncle Xander tell lots of stories about sleeping over in the summer holidays and having a fire on the beach, but Mum won't let me and Rory do it, it's not fair."

"We better be going now or the dogs get worried being away from Uncle Xander for too long. It was nice to meet you."

"Actually your Uncle said I could wander up and have a look at the castle if I got bored; I wonder if you could show me the path?"

"Oh sure, you just go a bit further along and you can see the side gate to the castle, come with us."

It literally was a hop skip and a jump from the beach, and the first building you came to be the gatehouse, which is where Bobby assumed Alexander Balfour, lived. However Mari told her in a very grown up fashion that they lived in the gatehouse – her, Mum, Dad and Rory and that Uncle Xander lived in one of the outbuildings next to the castle but Bobby would have to walk all the way up the gravel path. Just as Mari was explaining to Bobby where she would find her uncle an adult version of Mari with flame red hair came out of the gatehouse.

"Hello, can I help you?" said the small trim figured woman with the pale skin often associate with such flame hair, very pretty typically and authentically Scottish. She was wearing a beautiful full flower printed flowing sundress, and her skin was the colour of ivory.

 "This is the writer lady, Bobby, Mum. We met her on the beach, Uncle Xander said for her to call."

"Oh, how nice to meet you, I'm Morag, Alexander's sister in-law and these two who I presume you have met are my two children, Rory and Mari. Duncan, my husband is probably in the walled garden where he can usually be found when we all come in from school."

"I've told Bobby just to go up the path and she will find Uncle Xander."

"Yes indeed if you don't see him straight away just give a call for him he will be inside working, wearing himself out as usual. I keep telling him it's too much too soon, but hey don't listen to me I'm just an old hen as Xander would tell you. Just carry on up the path and shout and he'll appear."

"Thank you so much," Bobby replied. She also thanked the children just as they were letting the dogs off their leads, who, ran like the wind towards the castle where they knew for sure their master would be. Bobby waved bye to the little group and wandered up the gravel path towards the imposing castle. Which actually, she hadn't really had time to take in, being slightly distracted, by her conversation with the children. Children did so tell a perfect stranger all kinds of things thought Bobby, that they probably weren't supposed to but children were innocent of the adult hang ups such as privacy.

Chapter 9

Bobby followed the fast retreating dogs and once she had seen the door in which they ran to she slowed her pace in order to take in the sheer splendour and magnitude of the building. She had visited a castle once before but for some reason it was different being a visitor to an anonymous castle, but it was quite another thing to imagine it as someone's actual home. As she walked closer towards the door with her neck so far back in order to take in the sheer height of the building she almost bumped into a very dusty Alexander Balfour.

Standing at the open door complete with white dust mask and goggles covering his very hot and sweaty face, she jumped back apologising. She apologised not only for bumping into him but also it was obvious he was in the middle of an important job and she had interrupted.

"I'm so sorry I should have let you know, rang or something, you're busy I can tell, please don't let me interrupt as I know how annoying that can be."

"No, no please don't worry this is a never ending project, it wouldn't matter which day you had come to call I would be doing some job or other. Please, you are very welcome let me just get rid of these things and I'll give you a little tour, it's nice to see you."

He did look genuinely pleased to see her, as though he really didn't mind her calling thought Bobby, which helped her to be more at ease. She tried hard not to almost devour him with her eyes as he removed his goggles and mask and began to dust himself down. He wore what she presumed to be an ex-army bottle green t-shirt which showed every inch of his sinewy torso off to its leanest, and what looked like army fatigues' and he looked every bit the soldier.

"You found me alright then?"

"Well actually I found your nephew and niece on the beach and recognised them through the dogs. I made the mistake of thinking you were their father but they explained that only they and you are accepted by Tariq and Nazim."

"Well that's true they don't often leave my side, but they trust the children because they looked after them for me while I was in hospital."

"The children did say you're a soldier and were away in..?"

"I was a soldier, I was in Iraq. However I was invalided out, and Tariq and Nazim attached themselves to me when I was at

Camp Dogwood. The problem is when you leave for whatever reason, if you were fool enough to become attached to any animal it has to be shot. It's logistics you see. If every soldier posted in a foreign land attached themselves to an animal then when they ship out there would be hundreds of stray dogs left behind."

"But you had yours shipped home?"

"Yes, well I was fortunate enough as an officer to be able to bend the rules slightly and I certainly have plenty of space for two healthy, if a little odd looking animals. I am very fond of them and they kept me going through some very dark days."

"I'm sure they are very good company even though as you say their parentage is a little iffy, who cares and it's their devotion towards you that must be rewarding for you."

"Exactly. Now, enough of odd looking animals, come and look at what, in possibly ten years will become my home again. It was always mine and Duncan's home. Duncan is my older brother and should by all accounts have inherited the castle but he categorically refused to inherit the family pile. He lives with Morag and the children whom you have met, in the gatehouse. That must appear strange to you, that a person would rather live in a gatehouse rather then a castle.

"Living in a castle was, I won't deny it, fun as children but as the person who was responsible for the upkeep however, it was a financial drain and a nightmare. When it rained there were more buckets catching the water from the leaking roof than trees in a forest. In the winter it was so cold that it was more practical to sleep in your clothes or several layers of nightwear. This led Duncan and me to believe we were both conceived in the summer time? However it took a stint in the army to realise that I simply couldn't let the old place fall into ruin. Now that my wandering days are over, here I am attempting to put the old place back together again."

Bobby sensed there was so much more behind those brave words; she couldn't believe how much of himself and his family he had chosen to share with her. She felt him to be a private man or was that simply the opinion she had mistakenly formed on seeing his forced march along the dunes with his odd looking dogs. His stern face and lean frame, had led her to believe he was a totally different person, which she now scolded herself for judging him without knowing anything about him.

As they walked through the massive stone arched doorframe and into what Alexander called the Armoury Hall, which was where he was at present working on the beautiful wooden floor, sanding every inch of floor boarding until it brought back the beauty of the past. Alexander explained that the magnificent carved wall panels once held arms from the 16th and 17th century, pole–arms and roundels of Brown Bess muskets dating from around 1740, Lochaber axes from the latter part of the 18th century. Great tapestries adorned the remainder of the walls a huge fireplace sat centre stage and from the vaulted ceilings hung huge lanterns that would be lit by enormous candles.

"We have a lot of the armoury in storage simply to stop them from being damaged by damp. Father, bless him before he died spent every last cent replacing the roof so at least now the castle is watertight. It must have been a dilemma for him, whether to leave Duncan and me a tidy nest egg or replace the roof once and for all. It was always Fathers wish that a Balfour would live in residence again. He would be so happy and shocked to know it was going to be me. Oh we always knew Duncan never wanted the old place, and I had no time for anything except the army in those days.

It's strange how your priorities change in life….. Anyhow, it has become my life's ambition, no matter how long it takes and I think it will take a very, very long time, and lot of money, but even if it is a King's ransom, I will move back home again. A Balfour flag will fly once more."

"How absolutely wonderful," Bobby said. "I envy you, not only your ambition but your journey. You have a goal and I can tell that you will not give up until it's achieved."

As they wandered from room to room in various states of either repair or disrepair, it was clear that the castle was going to take a very long time to renovate and a great deal of money but Bobby envied Alexander the challenge; she could imagine how proud a person would be when they achieved their ambition.

"How on earth did you ever find each other when you were small, living in such a massive place, I wouldn't like to imagine how many rooms there are?"

"Well to be honest I've never really thought about it, I suppose in the region of about fifty, and a lot of those were never used even when we were children. I do know that the seven bedrooms were used occasionally at Christmas. There are technically six bathrooms however some of the fittings in most of them date back to the year dot and could never be used without causing a major catastrophe from some of the old pipe work.

"It's a wonderful house for playing hide and seek, and for riding your bicycle round the corridors. We were even allowed to roller skate along the corridors, the ones that weren't carpeted I must add, which was actually most of them. We did have a wonderful childhood, and we were so lucky, however it could be very cold and lonely."

"Lonely?" questioned Bobby.

"Well to be honest, although I loved to go to a school friend's house for tea and never give it a second thought that they had only one living room and one toilet, you were always in danger of looking like a rich snob, and yet nothing could have been further from the truth. In actual fact we were probably poorer than those who lived in a cottage.

"Their houses were always so lovely and warm and ours was always so bloody cold – even in the summer it wasn't much warmer. As for being rich, well after mum died who basically was the financial wizard and kept us all afloat, things went from bad to worse. So we didn't invite many children and of course we went to boarding school so we didn't really know many of the local children very well.

"You must be wondering why I want to restore the old place if it was that bad. But don't get me wrong it wasn't, that was a sign of the times, no central heating, no, mod cons. Now I intend to put in a multi fuel system, log burners in the corridors that will help the overall heating system to cope. It may look as though I haven't done a great deal however I have replaced most of the old pipe work which as you can imagine was a mammoth job. The electrics are next on the agenda, however I couldn't resist working on the entrance hall, and I am desperate to put the tapestries back on the wall and all the arms out of storage and back on display. It will feel less derelict once I move back in, if you see my meaning?"

"I do and I can totally understand, I think it's a wonderful and exciting project and I envy you… No I really do," Bobby repeated after he gave her a look of disbelief and the most memorable smile. It actually took Bobby by surprise because it transformed his taut features into a completely different person. It would have been impossible not to notice his very pronounced limp as they had walked around the length and breadth of the castle corridors. Although he tried his best not to show any discomfort, it would also be impossible not to notice his pained expression.

Bobby deliberately leaned against a convenient window seat or recess hoping that a few seconds rest between flights of stairs would give him a chance to rest his leg a little.

"I feel I must be holding you up from your work, and I know how irritating that can be."

"Oh, I wanted to ask about that. What kind of things do you write? I realise you are a writer but I didn't ask what, and would I know you, are you famous?"

"Oh no, I'm not famous and for my sins I write romantic fiction; however that has been to keep the wolf from the door, in the past so to speak. It is my intention to write something more substantial. Well that sounds very grand and I decided to give myself time while I'm at the cottage to write something more meaningful and more fulfilling, that's if I can. At the moment I seem to have dried up."

"Hearing you say 'cottage' makes me feel guilty all over again about the ….. err shack, which is what it is, it's simply for fishermen."

"I know, I know the children told me, please don't feel guilty, I love it, it's challenging but I love the solitude."

"Oh I see, well don't worry no one will disturb you here, I'll make sure of that."

"Oh no, no, I better explain, erm, last year I inherited a station, which included a house, waiting room and ticket office and wait for it a... *train!* Yes you heard right."

Alexander's face was a picture, just the same she supposed as if someone said they owned a castle.

"Well my two best friends and I moved from our student digs in Dumfries and they took on the train and the waiting room and turned one into a tea room and the other into a gift shop. My intention was to write without financial worries for a change. Until circumstances gave me the push I needed to get away for a while. Suddenly this was the wake up call I needed to remember what I had intended to do with my future after leaving university, not write romantic novels all my life.

"Listen thank you for showing me round your fantastic castle, I don't want to hold you up anymore, you have been too kind. When you pass the little cottage feel free to call in and I'll make you a coffee."

"I've enjoyed your company," replied Alexander, "and as long as I won't disturb you while you are writing I may take you up on that. But listen I'm stopping now anyway to take Tariq and Nazim for their walk so we'll walk you back."

The dogs were instantly at Alexander's feet upon hearing their names, although to be fair they had never been more than two feet away since Bobby arrived and although Bobby and Alexander chatted while walking down the gravel path the dogs obediently walked calmly at his side. It surprised Bobby how easily they chatted, how comfortable they both seemed in each other's company, two complete strangers. It also made Bobby feel slightly guilty as to the impression she had formed without rhyme or reason about the strange man and his even stranger looking dogs whom she had seen marching the beach. She decided she would be honest and tell him of her original opinion.

"I have a confession to make… The first night I saw you with Tariq and Nazim I thought you were very stern faced and on some sort of mission and I'm afraid I rather formed an opinion without even knowing you, and now I know that opinion was totally and utterly wrong. There I've said it, I think it wrong to form opinions on people who you don't really know yet I did just that, and it just shows how wrong you can be."

"Hey don't beat yourself up about it; we must look a strange looking bunch, me with my gammy leg and two weird looking dogs. And as long as we are making confessions then you're not the only one who forms opinions about people, I did the same with you. First of all I thought you were a fella, then, I thought you must be a runaway or something, so it just shows doesn't it, you have a perfectly innocent reason for being here."

They chatted easily as they reached the beach and arrived back at the cottage Bobby reminded him to call in whenever he wanted as after all she reminded him, it was his 'shack'.

Chapter 10

He thought she was a runaway! Well Bobby supposed that wasn't far from the truth, although it wasn't as though she were running from a crime or anything sinister, she told herself, so she wasn't really misleading him. Alexander, on the other hand had been very forthcoming, even mentioning his 'gammy leg' as he had put it. She had wanted to jump straight in and ask him about his leg injury, about his time in what Rory and Mari called 'the war'. It was strange to hear people speak of the war, to people like Bobby the war was something her father had been in, the Second World War and the First World War was where a grandparent would surely have been in.

After struggling for two days to find inspiration for something other than a love story Bobby's mind wandered back to her conversation with Alexander Balfour, about his lifelong ambition to become a soldier. And yet here he was apparently restoring his heritage and not appearing to miss his army career at all, or was that a front? Was he hiding from some mental trauma or Post Traumatic Stress Disorder? Seeing him each day, on his daily ritual of what could easily be mistaken for a gruelling schedule of self discipline, for what? To get fit? As a punishment? Why?

Bobby realised that sitting in her cabin by the sea, all alone with no inspiration was not producing her Magnum Opus. To be honest it was driving her mad, she wasn't used to having so much time to sit and think. She had been used to writing in a household where for one reason or another there was always a crisis. There was always a constant flow of human traffic and people apologising for disturbing her, yet that had never stopped her putting two lovers together, happy ever after. Yet here she was with as much peace and quiet as anyone could imagine yet she couldn't think of a single subject to write about.

Bobby knew she needed real life. She had never had to think about a story, they had simply popped into her head whilst washing dishes or tidying the very untidy living room where all three girls congregated which meant it usually had the remains of the previous nights takeaway, and various bottles or cans. When she lived at the house in Dumfries and was in the middle of a book her constant wish was that she had the time to tidy the room and work in a clinical space like a professional writer. Yet here she was, her pencils were almost standing to attention, with not a thing out of place and yet nothing, zilch, nada.

It was no good Bobby decided, she would have to create some real life, be normal. Yes she loved the surroundings, the sea, the sky, the Kevin free space, but she needed people, and who are people? Yup she thought, Alexander and when does he appear? Any minute now she thought pulling on her flat pumps and giving herself a quick scrutinise in the little mirror on the cottage wall.

By the time she saw the lone figure with his two odd looking companions trekking along the beach Bobby had made herself comfortable on the old dead tree which made a perfect vantage point. He was almost upon her before he actually saw her sitting there in fact, thought Bobby if the dogs hadn't made a tiny sound as they saw her sitting Alexander would have ran straight past her unaware of her presence. You had to wonder what on earth was going on in his mind for him to be as engrossed, or unaware of his surroundings as to actually run past a solitary human being sitting on a log on an empty beach, thought Bobby.

"Hey, you never called in for that coffee so I thought I'd visit you instead."

Alexander stopped and seemingly pulled himself out of his deep reverie, with a ready smile, which not evident at first, would suddenly light up his face giving him a totally different persona.

His serous face was a mask of concentration and controlled pain. Yet when he smiled he actually looked years younger, his eyes shone with his wide grin which brought out the boyish side of him, which Bobby felt sure he must have looked like when he and Duncan played together on this very same beach.

"Hello, sorry I was miles away."

"I could tell, I wish I had your concentration, in fact I'm beginning to wonder if I work better with a house full of people milling around. I'm not used to this much solitude, it seems to be killing my creative juices."

"I haven't called in because I thought I would be disturbing you but actually, I wanted to ask you something."

"Me? Oh fire away, I'm all ears."

"Well it was something you said the other day, you said you inherited a station and two of your friends had made businesses out of some parts, is that right?"

"Yes, my friend Suze made the train into a wonderful tea room, oh you should see it, and she has even put some old suitcases on the roof racks to give it authenticity. It's amazing, it would seem that the locals must have been desperate for some tearooms as she's even had to take on more staff. Penny, my other friend, turned the waiting room into a gift shop and apparently the customers who frequent the tearooms also buy at the gift shop, you know birthday presents, cards decorative items that sort of thing. They told me that the local bus had been diverted with my permission to become the bus terminus at the rail yard. This has doubled their trade in one fell swoop, as those getting on and off the bus use both the tearooms and the gift shop.

"Oh sorry, I'm rabbiting on and you wanted to ask me something."

"No, no you're not rabbiting; it's actually about that, that I wanted to ask. Listen if I finish my run and call on my way back, does the invitation still stand for coffee?"

"Of course."

"Then I'll see you shortly, say half an hour? Come on dogs mush, mush."

And off he went. Was it Bobby's imagination as he disappeared further down the beach, or was his run more like a jog than a forced march since he left her. Bobby decided it was far too nice a day to sit inside the cottage, she quite often sat at the ancient metal table and chairs which had been painted many different colours over the years and were now a sort of shabby chic, all chipped and scuffed off white colour, but which all seemed to blend in with the rustic ambience of the setting.

The table was set with a jug of chilled juice which she thought would be more appreciated after his jog. She had also found an ancient coffee pot which she had been using on the log burner which she found made a decent cup of coffee. She filled two old dishes with fresh water for Tariq and Nazim and pressed them into the sand so as not to spill out. She had just finished when she saw his figure hugging the shoreline splashing as he ran through the surf, no doubt keeping him cool in the warm wind. She had even found a packet of her favourite biscuits that she usually munched while typing, although not good for her figure they were often the only things she ate while working.

"Wow tea on the beach, I haven't done this since I was a child," Alexander panted as he plonked himself down on one of the chairs and the legs buried themselves a little deeper into the sand. The dogs seemed to instinctively find the cool water which Bobby had put slightly in the shade for them. Giving Alexander a large glass of chilled juice, she sat on the other chair enabling her to inhale the sheer scent of him. It was not unpleasant, he smelled faintly of shower gel and body heat. His hair was casually dishevelled making him look even more human and relaxed. This man thought Bobby was very complex, his persona was a very difficult one to gauge, his face was mobile one minute very serious and the next totally open.

Chapter 11

"So what was it you wanted to ask me? Fire away"

"Well it's a business question really; I'm just feeling the ground out in an attempt to find ways to… well, fund the restoration of the castle. And you gave me an idea the other day when you mentioned your friends. I have so many outbuildings and although I don't want to go down the route of opening up the castle to the public, which by the way my poor old dad would turn in his grave if I did. But the idea of, for example a tea room or a gift shop or something along those lines, anything really that would bring in some revenue which would help with the restoration, would be a dream scenario."

"I think that would be a marvellous idea, I did seem to walk past an awful lot of empty buildings which could be put to good use. When you look around at the various big houses that have had to turn commercial albeit reluctantly, the tearooms and the gift shops all do well. You can't fail to bring in revenue from food, you just have to provide basic facilities and it's all about advertising. Nowadays people look straight on the web to find places of interest for the day out, and usually what they have to offer and instructions on how to travel there.

"I think you couldn't fail to make money. The only fly in the ointment is… do you want visitors? How many weeks of the year would you want them? Could you find staff to work in the tearooms and the gift shop for example if that's the way you choose to go?"

"You seem to have a good grasp on what's needed. Would you have a walk back with me and take a look at the outbuildings and tell me what you honestly think?"

"I'd love to, I am no expert I might add, but my friends seem to have made a real good go of it. They had no previous experience, Penny did her degree in the finance area and Suze always intended to have her own tearooms but as for experience.. It was more or less trial and error and a lot of common sense."

"I won't be intruding on your writing will I?"

"Ha, chance would be a fine thing, I've never ever suffered from writer's block but I've come to the conclusion I would write better in the middle of Edinburgh Waverley Station. Oh don't get me wrong I'm loving every minute of the cottage, but for some reason I'm having difficulty putting pen to paper. No I would love to come and give my opinion for what it's worth."

"Come on then, no time like the present, and if I don't find some funds from somewhere I'm afraid the restoration will grind to a halt. I have my army pension of course but the work I've managed to accomplish so far came from my severance pay. So now I need some serious money in order to carry on, and carry on I will, even if I have to sell my soul.

"So how did your friends finance their businesses, they wouldn't come ready made, one must presume so it must have involved an outlay of cash?"

Seeing a look cross Bobby's face Alexander instantly felt he had inadvertently overstepped the mark.

"Oh I'm sorry was that indiscreet?. It never dawned on me and I have no right to ask such a question, forget I asked."

"No, no, please, honestly it's not a secret, it's what you said about selling your soul, and I also felt as though I had to do that very same thing, in order to finance the work which needed doing for the tearooms and the gift shop."

Bobby began to explain how the girls had always wanted to set up their own businesses and when the opportunity arose it made complete sense. She explained how she had inherited not only the house but as she said the rolling stock and waiting room etc. She then went onto explain how she had to approach the local bank. The village bank, where the manager was, it would seem the most important man in the village. It was he who held sway over all and every deal that needed finance. So to cut a long story short she felt she had to sell her soul to remortgage the station house in order to finance the alterations for the businesses.

This she explained was sound business practice as Penny had explained, and without risk as she trusted Penny and Suze completely to meet their repayments.

"But Kevin… erm Mr Hamilton, the manager not only didn't trust either Suze or Penny, he thought with the loan came a right to interfere. So beware, if you need to mortgage or finance the castle, go to someone who doesn't think it gives them the right to run your life for you."

A sudden look of understanding flitted across Alexander's face as if that explained something of Miss Lennox's sudden visit to his little shack on the beach.

"Ah I have no worries there, without sounding too stuffy, we are a very old family and although I may have no money, we do have connections. I know various people who would have the means to finance a deal if the percentage was right for them and if they thought the venture profitable."

As they chatted easily they eventually arrived at the first building Alexander wanted Bobby's opinion on. It was the old stables, it was very large and in remarkably good repair. In fact it still had straw left in some of the stalls.

"When was this last used?" Bobby exclaimed, "It almost looks as though someone has just taken the horses out for a hack? It's a fabulous building and surely you must have thought about this being a tea room or café? You wouldn't even need to change the name, it's absolutely perfect, Xander."

Bobby suddenly realised she sounded too familiar and apologised. "Sorry, I shouldn't–"

"No, no, don't be, my name sounds nice, er, really nice coming from you.. Bobby? Surely we are friends by now.... we must be close friends surely, after you have lived in my shack"

They both laughed at the inference and suddenly it was as though they both knew that they would be good friends.

"Well this building alone has more than wonderful possibilities, now lets see where you could have some facilities, I'm afraid with the public come the need for facilities."

"Well there is a ridiculously old outside toilet which was used for the stable lads and outside staff of yesteryear I may add, which could be updated fairly easily. I could actually do that, there isn't much to plumbing that I can't manage…. 'He says modestly,' " joked Alexander.

They walked further on towards yet another outbuilding, which apparently had been simply a grain or storeroom that had great possibilities; it was then that Bobby heard some activity going on behind the high wall of dark red stone. She could hear some sort of chopping noises.

"So, what's behind the wall then Xander?"

"Oh that's the walled garden, Duncan's domain; he loves gardening and keeps us all going with fresh vegetables and fruit."

As they turned the corner, sure enough there was an older more beefy version of Alexander Balfour; his dark hair flopped on his face while he shovelled the soil. He looked from his figure to be almost as tall as Xander and was also muscular however his frame was probably more through gardening than the physical training of the soldier.

"Hi elder brother, I've brought a visitor who wanted to watch you till the soil or whatever it is you're doing," Alexander said in an affectionate but sarcastic way to Duncan who looked up towards his younger brother.

"Elder brother indeed, don't think I couldn't catch you if I wanted to. That's why you do all that running, you're frightened I'm faster than you," replied Duncan in the same playful tone, as he stood up to his full height in order to ease the kink in his back, explaining.

"Hello, I'm sorry about the sibling, I'm Duncan Balfour and you must be the famous writer my little brother and my children told me about."

"Well I think famous is stretching the truth a bit far, although I am a writer, with what can only be described at the moment as writer's block. This place is so fantastically serene I find it difficult to get into the thrust of work. This is a wonderful garden Duncan. Is there only you or do you have help?"

Seeing the walled garden which was all neatly laid out and incredibly well organised with proper Victorian forcing pots and an incredibly long ancient Victorian green house, row upon row of cold frames, Bobby could only gaze in awe. She had never been a gardener but like most people she had been to country houses with the same type of layout, however there was usually a whole horde of gardeners who ran them.

"No, no, this is all my own work and it's the only part of the castle which I wanted and I love it. I spend my evenings and weekends in the garden and Morag loves it as well, although she likes the produce more than the actual digging. She deals with the soft fruits and anything she can make into a pie or a sweet with. I gather you've met Morag and the children who told me all about the writer who called the shack on the beach a cottage."

Saying this he gave such a laugh that Alexander groaned in embarrassment, saying not to mention it again. He already felt bad enough about charging anyone to stay in his childhood shack.

"But I love it, you just don't realise what us 'townies' class as a cottage, that's because you rich folk are used to the lap of luxury. Wonderful castles and cottages on the beach, all the fresh food you can eat while we poor town folk have to live in central heated homes and live off takeaways."

Duncan and Alexander laughed as they remembered how cold they used to be in the castle in the mid winter when all of their friends in the town had roaring fires in their small cosy living rooms. A takeaway was something Xander hadn't tried until he went away with his regiment, on a lad's night out, where beer and takeaway food was standard practice.

Duncan and Alexander knew instantly that Bobby understood their differences and yet revelled in making fun of them. That was how the instant rapport was to become a lasting friendship.

Chapter 12

"I'm asking Bobby about some money making ideas, which would impress the bank enough to lend me huge amounts of cash," Alexander explained to his brother.

"Well good luck there then," encouraged Duncan, "Morag and I are lowly teachers, so if Bobby can come up with a solution we're in."

"Ha, ha," laughed Bobby. "In my humble opinion you have at least two solutions right under your very noses."

Bobby looked for confirmation to go ahead with her off the cuff ideas which she stressed were literally her first thoughts and had by no means been costed etc.

"The first thing you have which won't take much converting are the stables, even the name wouldn't need to be changed. It's very 'in' now to go to places and eat 'a la shabby chic' and you couldn't get anymore authentic than the stables. With only the minimum of alteration you could have a working kitchen and with some updating for the toilet facilities and a damned good clean to satisfy health and safety. The actual horse stalls make ready made dining cubicles and you have a nice little earner there."

Bobby had been so busy doing her presentation talk, she hadn't noticed

Morag with her tray of tea and cakes approaching until a voice from the background said, "And I would love to run a tea room, instead of teaching children lessons in which they have no interest. Hi, I saw you all from the upstairs window and decided refreshments and introductions were in order."

As they all descended upon Morag's tray with thee most delicious looking scones, homemade cake and mugs of tea, they all sat on the ancient bench seats which lined the wonderfully warmed walls of the garden.

"Would you really rather work in the tea room Morag?" Alexander quizzed her.

"Yes, yes I would actually love it, you know how I love to bake for any event, but apart from winning a rosette you don't really get a lot of satisfaction from it. I've often thought whenever I've been into a tea shop, how I would run it."

"Well I never, I never knew that," Duncan said, while munching on one of Morag's excellent scones. "Well Morag if you think you would be happier doing that you should have said."

"Well teaching was fine before I had the children, but to be honest I've thought for a while I needed something more challenging."

"You really would run the tearooms Morag, if I went ahead and did the alterations?"

"Yes, Xander," she replied. "I would absolutely love to do it."

"And what else did you have in mind Bobby now that we have a taker for the tearooms?"

"Well of course there's more than enough room for a gift shop but the other thing that strikes me is that you have a market garden right here on your doorstep and you can't possibly eat all this produce in a million years, what on earth do you do with it all?"

"Well, I bottle a lot of the fruits and we give a lot of the vegetables away and we freeze quite a bit. To be honest a lot of it gets wasted," admitted Morag.

"What a terrible shame. For a start I could see the bottled fruit and marinated vegetables being very easily sold in delis in towns, but to be honest I wouldn't even do that; I would have a farm shop. I know it's not strictly a farm but you have the same products as they do and you grow them yourselves, so they are fresh and home produced.

"You have a gold mine here and you don't even know it. It takes a townie to see products that we could only dream about. I could never afford fresh asparagus or fancy bottled fruit in lovely gift wrapped kilner jars, labelled Balfour Castle. And as for the gift shop… well you have what all gift shops want and don't always have… a theme, you are a theme, you are Balfour Castle. Erm just stop me when you're bored you know, I do have a tendency to go on and on and I lived with two girl friends, who, used to bombard me with ideas; however I must say they are now quite successful by all accounts according to my last update."

"You're amazing Bobby," said Alexander, "and you make everything sound so easy. It all makes total sense when you say it.

After weeks of struggling along concentrating on the house, and putting off how and where I was going to find my next chunk of money, in order to do more renovating. You've offered us a solution which is within our grasp, and on our own doorstep."

"You will stay to dinner won't you Bobby?" Morag said in such a way that Bobby felt she couldn't refuse.

"I won't take no for an answer unless of course you're really busy working on your book."

"Amazing I may be at solving other peoples problems however I seem to be going through a writer's drought at present, it's all this peace and quiet I'm not used to it."

Seeing Morag's face, Bobby explained.

"Oh don't get me wrong I love it, but my creative juices don't seem to flow unless I'm under pressure. So if it's not putting you out at all, I would love to stay to dinner."

"Oh that's wonderful, that will mean that Xander will eat instead of putting the offer off until another day as he usually does, and he so desperately needs fattening up."

Just then Duncan and Alexander suddenly both began to laugh uncontrollably, so much so

Alexander was almost crying with mirth. Morag explained in such a way that only Bobby could hear.

"Would you look at that? You're a magician, I don't know what you've done to him, but that's the first time Xander has laughed since he came home from Iraq. I can see a change in him just in the last week or so and today when you were explaining about the tearooms, he was watching you with such interest and brightness, like the old Xander before he went to that terrible place. You do him the power of good Bobby; I sense major changes at Balfour Castle."

Morag began to collect the tea tray asking Bobby if she would help her carry them back to the gatehouse cottage. It was obvious that it was simply a ruse to chat to Bobby without Alexander overhearing but Bobby was quite happy to go along as she was almost as curious about him as Morag was about her.

Morag gave a low shout to the brothers who seemed deep in conversation.

"We're just off with the tray, dinner will be at six sharp, Duncan mind you're back in time to wash your hands."

The men hardly noticed the women had gone as they carried on their conversation about old times which seemed to amuse them very much.

"Do you know before Xander went to Iraq he would never, ever have entertained restoring the old place? army, army, army, that's all he ever cared about. From being a boy that's all he ever wanted was to join the Black Watch, The Royal Highland Regiment, like his father and grandfather before him. He only agreed to go away to university on condition he went to Sandhurst to become an officer straight after.

"He worked so hard… Officer, then a Captain, then a Major! He was sent to Camp Dogwood, of all places where he almost lost not only his leg but also the best part of his hip. He's had so much surgery, they wanted to remove the leg but he wouldn't agree. They told him he wouldn't walk again, that he would be in a wheelchair for the rest of his life, but he's proved them wrong. And now God love him he hates the very mention of the word war!

"Poor man he has such demons, such mood swings, he drives himself onward and onward like a man possessed. We try not to interfere but just to be there for him but it breaks Duncan's heart. They were the closest of brothers, they still are and when he comes through this dark tunnel he's in, they will be again I'm sure of it.

"Listen to me going on and on, I'm sorry you don't want to know all this, you just being a visitor and all. But I wanted to talk to you about this tearoom business – did you mean it? Would it work? Would you be here to give us a bit of advice and that? It's just I've never seen Xander looking so much happier and more positive and it doesn't take brain of Britain to see why."

Morag looked squarely at Bobby. "He's taken with you, you seem to have broken through his shell. Don't get me wrong he was always outgoing and friendly a real gentleman but since he has been back, he won't cross the doors and he buries himself in the castle working and working. This idea of yours seems to have caught his imagination and to be really honest, mine as well. I would really love to run a little tea room, and what better place than on my door step."

"I don't know about Xander being taken with me, I think maybe we've sort of hit it off at the time when we both need some distance between our past lives. Without realising it of course, but yes, I really do think the tearooms would take off and to be honest I think the market garden is a wonderful idea. The garden needn't simply be a seasonal thing, Duncan tells me you bottle fruits and peppers and stuff, and I'm sure he grows winter vegetables as well? I have absolutely no doubt that both ventures would do well.

"As for me staying, I am definitely here until July and who knows, nothing is set in stone. I am also positive my friends in Hollybush, with their newly formed businesses, would offer any practical help they could as they are both actually 'living the dream' so to speak!"

Chapter 13

A crunch of tyres on the gravel
outside the gatehouse heralded
children's excited voices and shouts
of thanks and see you tomorrow's.
Like a whirlwind of bustle and
sound in rolled Rory, weighed
down with sports bag, school
satchel and what looked as though it
had once been a school sweater, all
crumpled up in his hands, closely
followed, by Mari who was slightly
less untidy but just as weighed
down with school paraphernalia,
both calling "Hi" as they burst in.

"Oh, hi Bobby, you here to see
Uncle Xander?"

Morag cut out the explanations by telling both children that Bobby was staying for dinner, which was going to be at six so if they wanted to play out they only had forty five minutes to do it.

Rory said very excitedly that both he and Mari were rebuilding the Balfour Battler which when translated apparently was a go-cart they had found in one of the outbuildings.

"It used to belong to Dad and Uncle Xander and they said we could have it if we did it up."

Rory told Bobby excitedly, there is going to be a go-cart race on the last day of term so we're doing it up and Mari is my co-driver, we're allowed to do that even though she's a girl and she's just as good as any boy and I suppose it is half hers after all.

"I should think so, aren't I doing half the work, and I'm making the stencils so that we can paint the name back onto the side?" Mari said indignantly as though Rory was doing her a favour in agreeing to let her be co-driver.

"Change your clothes, dump your PE stuff in the washer and don't forget to come in when I shout for tea, ok?"

They both chimed in unison "Yes Mum".

"Come with us Bobby, please you have to see this it's really cool, please come," Rory pleaded with Bobby, and Morag indicated it was totally up to her as the meal was a casserole and she wouldn't need any help as there was only the table to set. So the little trio of excited bodies almost ran towards one of the outbuildings. "This," Rory said proudly, "is where we are working on it. Just wait until you see it, it's great isn't it Mari?"

"Oh it's going to be lovely when it's painted, and I'm doing the painting and the stencilling of the name on the side, The Balfour Battler... Imagine that?"

Rory and Mari pulled open the old wooden doors and pulled out this 'battle bus' of a go-cart which had obviously been made for fairly large boys and was a sturdy looking craft if only a bit on the beat up side. The wheels looked as though they had had a crash or two. But as Rory explained they had those to remove and straighten out a little but they would be fine after that. The frame was made from an old metal frame of some sort with wooden planks fastened onto it. Sitting in the middle was what looked like a very large orange box which was obviously where the driver and passenger sat. Judging by the size of the seating positions Duncan and Alexander must have been similar ages to Rory and Mari in order to fit inside.

The children's excitement was palpable, they clearly saw something far more sophisticated than Bobby did and she envied them their childhood innocence.

"Well, isn't it great?" Rory's face was aglow with pride, so Bobby had to wonder what state it had been in for him to be so pleased with their progress.

"It's fabulous, I haven't seen such a good go-cart since… well, ever, mine always consisted of an old pram frame and four pram wheels and a plank of wood to sit on and I always managed to crash before the end. Yours will probably be the best one in the race, especially once you do all the stencilling Mari."

"Have a sit in it Bobby, go on, go on, you'll see how cool it is, go on have a go."

Bobby hadn't the heart to disappoint them especially Rory who obviously saw some sort of racing car in his world.

"But surely I'll break it, it's not made for my weight, I can see how good it is from here."

But Rory wasn't having any of it, he was so proud he wanted Bobby to see it from the driver's perspective.

"No, no, this was made to take Dad and Uncle Xander's weight so you won't be too heavy, go on, please Bobby."

"Oh, ok, but I'll try and not put all my weight on it, just in case, because I think your Dad and Uncle Xander were much smaller when this was made."

Bobby very gingerly climbed over the top and sort of plonked her bottom into the box shape and dangled her legs over the front while Rory handed her the rope which had to be changed for a new piece but it would give her a better idea, he said. Bobby was sitting in this position with the rope in her hands pretending to be rushing down a hill when Duncan and Alexander popped their heads around the door.

Seeing Bobby squeezed into the wooden seat, legs all akimbo pretending to race down a hill brought on such a fit of the giggles from Duncan and Alexander, who were obviously in a giggly mood, that even the children joined in. So much so that as Bobby attempted to climb out and found she was stuck which brought on even more fits of giggling from everyone even Bobby, who at first thought them very unkind to laugh at her dilemma, but couldn't help but see the funny side of a full grown woman stuck in a go-cart with her legs dangling over the front.

"Well I'll say one thing for you Bobby; you really throw yourself into any project no matter how small. Here let me help you out there Miss you look a little 'stuck'!"

Duncan and Alexander took one each of Bobby's hands and began to pull her like a wish bone but as her legs had nothing to grip onto and her bottom appeared to be stuck in the box they had to use all their strength giving the impression she was some sort of huge obese woman who had got stuck in her seat. This of course reduced everyone to tears of laughter so much so that no one had heard

Morag calling them all for dinner, so she had come to investigate. Morag's face was a picture of pure joy at seeing everyone laughing so naturally and with real mirth and one glance at Bobby's predicament helped her see why and joined the hilarity of the ridiculous situation she had got herself into.

The evening meal, when they all eventually got sat down, was a most pleasant affair and they were all in such good spirits. Especially Duncan and Morag who were so happy to see Alexander laugh and joke, the way he always did before he went away to Iraq, which they feared had changed him forever. After helping Morag with the dishes Bobby made her excuses but also her grateful thanks for a wonderful evening.

"Oh my dear," said Morag, "don't thank us, we have you to thank, being stuck away and cut off from civilisation we don't often get to see anything so funny as you stuck in that go-cart, that's something I'll never forget." "Me either," chimed in Duncan. The children had long since gone to bed but they had invited her to come again as they had had great fun although they hadn't managed to get any repairs to the go-cart done.

Alexander immediately stood up as did Tariq and Nazim and the whole motley crew said their goodbyes and made their way towards the beach. Bobby instinctively knew that once they were out of earshot Duncan and Morag would discuss the change in Alexander that was obvious for even Bobby to see this evening.

"Well you certainly know how to give everyone a good time," grinned Alexander.

"Erm, well I think you could have phrased that a little better, but we have had a good laugh though haven't we? The children are wonderful. I didn't realise how little children needed to make them happy. They are absolutely one hundred percent sure that their go-cart is going to win the race, Rory sees it as a Ferrari or McLaren that simply needs a slight paint job. And Mari is equally as enthusiastic, she thinks by painting the Balfour Battler on the side it will make it superfast. Oh don't you wish you could go back and be that innocent again?"

Alexander had a sudden distant look in his eye as he agreed wholeheartedly that he did. Bobby could see the struggle going on in his face; he didn't want to spoil a perfectly good evening by thinking of things that had spoilt his innocent view of life.

"Did I tell you?" Alexander said in attempt to save the happy mood that he had enjoyed all evening, in fact since Bobby had arrived. "Duncan and I used to race that go-cart down the corridors in the house, but don't you dare tell Rory or Mari that or they'll want to do the same. Father helped us make it, the frame is off an old dolly off a rail line, you know the kind of thing they use when they are running up and down the line making repairs. Well Father managed to purloin one… so he told us," Alexander recalled, tapping his finger to his nose.

"And all three of us thought, when it was first made and painted, that it was brilliant, we were the battling Balfour brothers… Ah those were the days. We never knew how lucky we were in comparison to some children."

Bobby could see his mind dragging him back to unhappier times and she wanted to pull him back to the present, but she didn't know him well enough yet, or feel she had the right to speak of the horrors he had seen. All she could do was give him time, time to dip into the past then back again if he could. That must be why, Bobby thought, when he marched up the beach without even noticing she was there, it was because he was faraway in a different world, a world where he couldn't help and now they couldn't help him mend himself.

But I could thought Bobby, it was obvious this afternoon and tonight how happy he could be, it's still in there, it's just temporarily buried under so much bad stuff. Bobby decided there and then, she wanted to stay here for the remainder of the summer. She wanted to get to know not only Alexander but the rest of his family. Help them with the tea room, the market garden and the gift shop if they wanted her. There was nothing stopping her, the girls were paying rent which was keeping the bank happy, and she didn't need much and she had her own little nest egg. And let's be honest she thought to herself, I'm loving it here, and… Well, she let herself take a sideways glance at Alexander as he wandered along beside her, well… She liked him… very much and would like to help him regain his life, if she could.

By the time they reached the cottage the last rays of the evening light were sinking below the horizon, which had always made Bobby think the sun fell down behind the sea when she was a child. Alexander almost forgot to stop, as his thoughts were so far away, but something about her stillness brought him back. As he turned to look at Bobby his eyes were a mixture she thought, of sadness, confusion, appraisal of her? Did she see that or was that her imagination?

"Well this it, my cottage on the beach, that I hired this from a very rich and posh land owner you know!"

"Please don't, I will forever be ashamed of your description of the shack as a cottage and I feel you deserve a refund. I only rented it out in an effort to begin being sensible and attempt to earn some money. But… I'm so glad you made the mistake and came anyway, I'm so glad you're not a fisherman. And if you can spare the time and only if we won't intrude with your writing, I think we unanimously would like your help and advice on how to make the first step in beginning our Balfour Castle enterprises?

"And I enjoy your company." This part was said in a bit of a rush.

Suddenly Alexander leant forward and kissed Bobby fleetingly on the cheek before saying goodnight, and then he was off down the beach into the distance, not marching but jogging. Yes, definitely jogging.

Chapter 14

When Bobby woke up the following morning with the warm rays of sunshine on her face she suddenly wanted to jump up and go for a swim, deciding she could always shower later. The sudden urge was the result of her mood, she felt rejuvenated, full of energy and a feeling of inner calm about finding an idea for a story. It seemed to come to Bobby in a flash, that life was going on all around her and didn't they say that art mirrored life? So, if you believed that then there was a story unfolding and would manifest itself just as her romantic stories had in the past, she simply must let it happen and try not to force it.

She ran down towards the surf in her cut off denims and old vest top which had seen better days but was fine for swimming in, and ran head long into the curling white surf, gasping as the icy water took her breath away. Her skin which had been warm from the early morning sun soon became chilled and after a brief but furious swim in the swell of the sea she made her way back to the warmth of the beach. Laughing out loud at how chilly it had been but feeling very brave to have made the effort Bobby staggered back towards the cottage.

It didn't take her long to warm through as the morning was perfect, not a cloud in the sky or a breath of wind. She sat at the old metal table outside the cottage and had her breakfast of toast and coffee. Subconsciously waiting for the odd looking trio she had come to know and began to care about without knowing quite when.

After a while it became apparent that Alexander and the dogs were not going to appear this morning and try though she might Bobby couldn't help wondering why? It was then she came up with the idea of pretending to be a visitor to the castle, she would take her note pad and work out from the entrance the logistics of how and what a visitor would want on their arrival. That, thought Bobby was constructive and would also give her a reason to be at the castle, which is where she seemed to want to gravitate towards.

Taking her battered old car she drove out of the dunes and back towards the main road. She pulled up outside the castle gates and made a note of what a visitor would expect which was a parking area of sorts. This could be cheaply and easily achieved with some rail and post fencing around a gravelled area. She then walked in past the gatehouse and on towards the outbuildings which is when she heard the hammering coming from the shed where the children kept the go-cart. As Bobby approached the shed the first thing she noticed was Tariq and Nazim curled up on an old blanket solemnly watching the proceedings.

"Hello," she called to them. Both dogs did rise and come towards her in a greeting but then settled down almost as quickly. Rory and Mari looked up from their labours of hammering wheels and painting saying,

"Hi Bobby, you haven't come to sit in our go-cart again have you because we've taken the wheels off for painting."

"No, I haven't, and don't remind me, I won't live that down for a long time getting my bottom stuck in a car seat. I see you have Tariq and Nazim that's unusual isn't it I didn't think they ever left your Uncle's side?"

"They don't but he's gone to Glasgow and whenever he goes to Glasgow they stay with us."

"Oh, I didn't know, he never mentioned it. Poor doggies they look so forlorn whenever he leaves them don't they?"

"Do you know it's suddenly dawned on me that it's Saturday, I seem to have lost track of the days since I've been staying in the cottage. Is your Mum home?"

"No she's gone shopping but Dad's in the garden."

"Oh well I'll nip and see him, I have some ideas I'd like to run by him. Bye, see you later, bye dogs."

As Bobby walked towards the garden her thoughts tried so hard to concentrate on the layout of the buildings and what should come first or second for the incoming visitors, but she couldn't help but wonder what had taken Alexander away in such a hurry, he hadn't mentioned anything the previous evening. She suddenly had a thought that maybe he'd gone to see one of his banker friends to see if he could rustle up some finance. Of course thought Bobby, that's what it'll be. Content with her own explanation her thoughts returned to the layout of the coffee shop, market garden produce and gift shop.

She decided that if she were a visitor who had just driven however many miles to get there the first thing they would want is the loos then the coffee shop. So it was obvious they should come first, then the building directly on the otherside of the garden wall should be the market garden produce, this would show it was grown right there on the premises. Then after that, would be the gift shop, where people may want to buy a souvenir of their visit.

It was then that she heard a cry of pain from over the garden wall, who she presumed was Duncan as it was followed by a curse of.

"Stupid bucket, who put that there?"

"Well it certainly wasn't me." Bobby said as she popped her head round the wall, laughing at Duncan who was hopping around in obvious discomfort.

"Oh I'm sorry, I hope you didn't see the blue air a minute ago, I nearly broke my big toe on that… Never mind that, hello and what brings you up here this fine morning? –Oh what am I saying,

Xander obviously, well emm, I'm afraid he's gone to Glasgow."

"Yes, err yes the children told me, they had Tariq and Nazim so I thought he must have gone out, he never mentioned it last night."

Bobby tried to say this as though it wasn't a problem and she wasn't really that bothered. However Duncan wasn't fooled.

A slight cough escaped from Duncan indicating her was trying to find a way to say something he found difficult.

"Erm, he didn't know he was, well, erm he got a phone call and all I know is when he gets a phone call he suddenly ups and goes to Glasgow. I have no idea where or why he goes and I don't feel its right to ask him. Erm that's another thing I better warn you about, when he comes back he seems to have sunk back into that depression which seems to come over him at times."

"Oh please I'm just a visitor, I have no right to expect Alexander to be here just for me, so please don't worry on my account."

This was said far too quickly and it was obvious to both Duncan and Bobby that 'the lady doth protest too much'.

Duncan left his spade and went to sit on one of the bench seats as they had the first time they had met and indicated for Bobby to do the same.

"Listen, I have eyes, I can see, within a couple of weeks of you being here Xander has come out of his protective shell. And last night he exceeded all our wishes and it was like the old Xander was home and sitting at our dinner table again. I know that's thanks to you, I'm not going to stick my big nose into yours or Xander's business, but any fool can see you make him happy.

I must warn you though, that when he comes back from Glasgow he is almost the way he was when he arrived back from hospital. It's as though the whole world was sitting on his shoulders and Xander takes his responsibilities very seriously. I just don't want you to be upset if he appears to not even notice you. Sometimes he doesn't eat for days when he comes back, he just goes into the castle and works and works until he emerges from his self torment.

"But you couldn't know Xander when we were younger, he is a lovely guy. Kind, thoughtful, he would lay down his life for you… That's his problem…

"Oh don't let me put you off; you have been such a tonic for all of us. Morag is really excited about the tearooms and I would love to do the market garden. You are still interested in helping aren't you Bobby, because we would really love it if you could find it in your busy schedule?"

"Busy schedule, me, listen I've just been planning the route for the visitors and making notes, of course I'm still interested. And Duncan… I'm not a tender flower that can't deal with real life, and I can see that Xander is hurt inside, and his memories are still tearing him apart, and if I can help in anyway then I'm in.
Besides, I've never had as much fun, and I get to live on the beach in my very own beach hut, what more could a person want?"

Bobby had made extensive notes and made a serious attempt to cost out how much she thought each individual project would cost. Estimating was a skilled job though and hers was only guesswork, but after talking to Suze and Penny on the phone she had been reassured that if she needed any help then they would be up like a shot.

It turned out that Penny was now dating the electrician who had done the alterations to the gift shop, and Suze had dated the guy from the Antique shop more than a few times

Chapter 15

It was the evening of the third day of Alexander's absence. It had been a particularly hot day and Bobby had spent most of her time on the beach. She had walked the shore line each day when Alexander had been away and had mindlessly collected chunks of driftwood with which she decided on the spur of the moment she would use to make an evening bonfire on the beach.

Bobby decided she felt like Robinson Crusoe living off the beach as she ate her baked potato which she had placed in the hot glow of the fire earlier. She thought to herself that life couldn't get much better than this except…. A mate would help, she couldn't live on the beach forever without a mate, and even Crusoe had Friday. Suddenly on the edge of the surf in the almost pitch dark Bobby thought she saw a figure moving along the shoreline. Amazed that she felt no fear, this heavenly place felt secure and safe and something stirred deep inside as she hoped upon hope it was Alexander.

The figure began to come closer and veered up the beach towards her little campfire and she saw the figure, a hood almost covered his face but his low slung fatigues left her in doubt that the figure was that of Alexander. His faithful dogs at his side as he arrived and the glow of the fire shone on his taut, tired face. There was something else, something which shocked Bobby and melted her heart, so much so she wanted to jump up and hug him close. She could see the silver streaks of tears which had long since dried but were still evident on his cheeks.

Playing his absence down Bobby went into her entertainment mode in an attempt to make it less painful for both of them.

"Hi, friend, would you like to sit at my campfire? I have a red hot charred baked potato if you're hungry? I'm sure they must be good for something, the charcoal at least makes your teeth shine white."

"Erm thanks', but no thanks, I think I'll give that a miss, but I'll take you up on the offer of the campfire, it looks real welcoming to an old cowpoke like me."

"It was such a beautiful night I just couldn't stay inside, you know?"

"Yes, that's what the shack is for really and Duncan and I used to sit outside with a campfire when we were young. Oh we had some good nights on the beach, we were so lucky; I never knew how lucky we were. I hadn't a clue how other people had to live their lives and all we had to complain about was the leaking roof and no heating, poor little rich boys."

"Hey don't beat yourself up about it, you said yourself you weren't rich or privileged, you weren't responsible for the fact that you lived in a castle and I've never met a more grounded family than you and Duncan. Listen, I lived in a three bedroom semi with central heating, and we had a car which even when I was young was a relative luxury compared to some other families. I met all kinds at university, rich poor, spoiled; life is not always about what you have, it's how you use it. And what kind of a person it makes of you, and from what I can see both you and Duncan are 'really nice fellows',"

The last was said in a humorous way so as to lighten the mood, making it easier for Alexander to feel less guilty about his past, which seemed to be what was eating him up. He seemed to feel he had, had a privileged background, which left him feeling weighed down with guilt.

With only the glow from the fire lighting the small space around the two figures, it was easier to talk in the half-light. It felt like having a conversation with the light out and somehow it made it easier to say what you wanted without embarrassment.

"I missed you… when you went away…"

"Did you? ...I had to go… had to go to Glasgow… But it's fine now… For a while."

"I thought maybe you had gone to see one of your rich banker friends? About a loan?"

"A loan…?"

"A loan, to start the tearooms and the market gardens and things?"

"Oh sorry, I'm with you. Sorry I was miles away. No, no but I will, I think it a wonderful idea of yours. But would you stay for a while? Would you be here?"

Bobby had dragged the massive old tree trunk up from the beach during the day, then later as she had lit the fire she had laid a blanket on the sand and as she sat with her back resting against the drift wood warming her hands from the heat off the fire. She indicated for Alexander to come and sit with her on the ground.

He moved down onto the blanket and they sat for a minute in companiable silence before Bobby said.

"Would you like me to stay?"

"Yes," was all he said, the dogs lay quietly and calmly just as he was sat, calm, almost motionless with his hands resting on his legs.

Bobby reached down and laid a hand on top of one of his and said quietly, "Then I'll stay."

They sat not talking but completely happy with each other's company until the fire turned to embers and the chill began to invade their bodies.

"Listen you should be in bed now, how about you invite me for coffee in the morning after I finish my run?"

This was said almost in the tone that Bobby knew as 'normal' for Alexander. He pulled her up from their sitting position and the dogs were instantly alert to their masters every move, he leaned into Bobby and held both of her arms as though he wanted to kiss her but didn't want to get too close, then his lips, firm and strong were drawn towards Bobby's soft yielding mouth. She hadn't dared think about it but she knew she had waited since the moment she'd seen him on the shoreline, for this moment. She so wanted to pull him close and hold him until whatever it was that hurt him had gone. But for now she had to be content with the kiss, the kiss that was like a soft explosion going off in her stomach. His lips were gone… And so was he, gone into the darkness and his little entourage with him.

Chapter 16

The next morning when Bobby looked down to the shoreline and saw his familiar figure her heart leapt. She made no attempt to listen to the little voice in her head which urged her to remember that this was not everyday life; this was some sort of summer dream. No she wouldn't listen to the voice because she simply wanted to enjoy the day, something she had never been able to do, she had gone to university, worked hard gained her degree, then worked and worked to keep her head above water. While lots of her friends took gap years and travelled around the world she stayed at home as she always had a book to finish or the rent to pay. So she told herself, to hell with it, this is my gap year.

As once again it was a beautiful morning Bobby had laid the coffee and French rolls outside on the old table. She could tell by the lift of his shoulders that Alexander was feeling more like his old self. Strange she thought, I hardly know him yet I can sense by the way he runs or marches whether he is depressed or not.

"Hi, ah breakfast alfresco, you can read me like a book, I'd much rather be outside than in."

How strange he should say that, it was as though he had read her thoughts.

"Listen I hope you don't mind but I did a dummy run as though I were a visitor and have got some notes and rough costs for the alterations. Now I'm no estimator and they are only rough guesses but I've also had a few thoughts on how you should lay things out… Erm that is if you don't mind, and don't feel I'm taking over?" Bobby said, suddenly looking up directly into his smiling face.

"No, no that's great."

Alexander was smiling at Bobby's enthusiasm and as she looked up from her notebook he gave her the full force of his wonderful smile.

"What? What have I said?"

"Nothing, you're wonderful do you know that? You hardly know us at all, you paid money to stay in our shack on the beach and now you're helping sort my finances out. When will you get a chance to write your book? I feel guilty taking over all your spare time like this."

"Oh please don't be, I love every moment of it. I just reminded myself that while everyone else had a gap year going round the world and seeing wonderful sunsets, I was probably writing some happy ending for two romantic lovers to walk off into the same sunset. I really am enjoying myself now Xander, really."

Bobby looked into his face as she said it and she could see by the rise of his chest and the smile in his eyes, that he realised this also included his company, which made him grin like a teenager. And not only Bobby but any fool could see those feelings were reciprocated by him, as yet they were slow but burning embers, but what will be will be. thought Bobby.

"Will you promise something Bobby?"

"If I can"

"I want you to be a friend of not only me, but the family and so from now on, please don't feel you need an excuse to come up to the castle. If you don't arrive then I will assume you are writing but please come when ever you feel like it. I really want to go ahead with the tea room and the market garden, but mainly I would like you to be a friend."

"Thank you, Xander I would really like that."

Bobby suggested she walk back with him and explain her thoughts and show him her notes. Explaining the only fly in the ointment was funding and if he had any connections in the banking industry now would be a good time to rekindle old friendships.

"You are shameless Miss Lennox although hold on, so am I charging for the rental of a shack on the beach. And by the way that stops as of now."

"No Xander, I refuse to stay if you don't take my rent, I'm staying because I want to and I'm getting more than I bargained for, I'm having the time of my life so you will not refund my money or I will be offended. I know how difficult it can be taking money off your friends however, business is business. Oh my God I sound like creepy Kevin…"

"Who on earth is creepy Kevin when he's at home?"

"Ha, at home is where he is, and that was the trouble, he was the bank manager who organised the loans for Suze and Penny, do you remember me telling you about him? He became a little too possessive over me, in fact he became a bit of a pest which is why I did a runner."

"Really, it was because of him that you ran…. Ah ha so I was right you were a runaway? Ha ha I knew it was a bit strange a lovely girl like you coming to live in the middle of nowhere in a fisherman's shack."

"Don't get carried away, yes I did do a runner and yes you were right, well partly, I really did want to write and I couldn't write with his constant interruptions and he was becoming increasingly… Ugh."

Alexander actually stopped smiling for a moment and his eyes flashed with anger.

"Did he really bother you Bobby? He didn't get out of hand did he?"

"No, no, nothing I couldn't handle, no he just thought he had the right to more in my life than simply being the bank manager. Suze and Penny thought it was just a crush he had on me and if I'd needed any protection from him don't you worry they were my own personal Rottweilers.

Anyway unless your bank manager is a woman after your body then you should be fine, but if it is, then I'll protect you don't you worry!"

Alexander seemed to relax a little and gave a little laugh saying the last time he had spoken to the bank, the manager was definitely a man but if there had been any change he would take her up on her offer of protection as long as she promised to do the same.

"You have my word on it."

Changing the subject, Bobby got down to explaining her ideas.

"You need some professional estimates, but I actually don't think there is any major building work needs doing to be honest Xander, I bet you and Duncan and maybe a jobbing builder or handyman could do most of the work. That would save a lot of money, money that can be spent on fitting the tearooms and the stocking the gift shop. You need to think about what kind of merchandise you want to advertise your shop and coffee shop.

You know what I mean for instance the Balfour flag or coat of arms, on say, mugs and tea towels you know the type of thing?"

"My God, Father would turn in his grave if he knew what I am about to do, however that's the reason the castle is a ruin because he wouldn't think of any commercial venture. Well I think it makes sense, if turning the grounds into small businesses means I can live in the castle again then I'm all for it.

"Morag is so excited about the tearooms; she was even thinking about putting her notice in before the school breaks up for the summer to give them a chance to find a new teacher. I think she has secretly wished for a chance like this but never dreamed she would get the chance.

"Actually I do know a small family builder in the village who may be interested in the work and as you say between Duncan and myself and you… don't think because you're a woman you're getting away with it." Alexander flashed Bobby that lovely smile which turned her knees to jelly, saying she would be the organiser in charge of ordering materials and merchandise etc.

"Which makes you admin, ok?"

"Ha, ha, ok, it makes a nice change for me to do something real for a change. You do realise my life is fictional, that's what I do all day, every day – create fiction, so this will be a reality check for me."

Chapter 17

In the weeks that followed group meetings would be held depending on the weather of course, in either Duncan's garden, catching the last rays of sunshine and the warmth from the walls as they all sat around a makeshift table, or in Morag's cosy kitchen, however at all meetings gallons of tea and enough homemade scones to feed a regiment were consumed.

They had managed to bring onboard the local builder McKinley who Duncan remembered had once been handyman-come-gardener for the Castle in the days when they could afford one. He had agreed a price which to be honest seemed more than reasonable, he had also agreed that if Duncan and Alexander did most of the labouring then he would take that into account.

Bobby had researched prices for fittings and fixtures, such as tables and chairs for the tearooms. She had been advised by Suze where to go to buy a second hand fridge cabinet for cake and scone displays, also the coffee machines were exorbitant new and whilst doing her own research Suze had found a wonderful place which reconditioned old machines and also guaranteed them for twelve months. Penny had explained it was much cheaper to simply have a joiner make your gift display cabinets than buy them as she had found to her cost, especially if your room is an awkward size.

At the end of each meeting Alexander walked Bobby back to the cottage, with Tariq and Nazim as usual walking silently beside them. As they reached the cottage it had become the most natural thing to part with a gentle none committal kiss before Alexander would jog off into the night. This in some relationships would have seemed very tame; however Bobby knew that for Alexander who was emerging from his own pit of depression, commitment was something he found very difficult.

The next meeting proved to be one of celebration after Alexander had approached his father's bank in Edinburgh, with a business plan which they had all jointly put together. Their plan had included not only the cost of the building work, fixtures and fittings, but also the projected figures from expected sales and visitor numbers. They included a plan for the use of the Balfour name for advertising products. These products would of course be sold not only in the gift shop but would also be sold on line at some stage, to for example, the Americans who love anything with Tartan on it.

As Alexander produced the bottle of champagne from behind his back a great cheer rang from the group to which even the dogs jumped at the sudden squeals from the two women.

"The bank has approved the loan, I think it was more out of respect for Father, which is not to say our business plan wasn't first class I might add. He did ask some pretty searching question's which thanks to all concerned I was able to give satisfactory answers to."

When the happy group broke up for the evening with starting dates agreed upon and orders confirmed Alexander and Bobby as usual leaving a buzzing Morag and Duncan still talking of their future commitments. It was then that Alexander put out his hand and took Bobby's casually as though it was the most natural thing in the world, as though they had always done it. They walked slowly towards the cottage and the evening was still warm even though it was almost dark. As they arrived at the cottage instead of a slight brush of the lips as usual, Alexander pulled Bobby into his arms, and as she looked up into his face she saw something that she hadn't seen before, a sort of calmness, the kind you feel when you take a deep breath and you are contented.

His whole face seemed to smile as he spoke softly into her long black tresses of hair.

"What is it about you, sweet Bobby? What is it that makes

everything seem all right? What is it that gives me the courage and the strength to go on; when that was the last thing I wanted to do only a few months ago?"

He breathed a huge sigh and crushed Bobby closer so she could feel the taut muscles beneath the thin material of his old army t-shirt which he seemed to wear as a constant reminder of a time he could never forget or put behind him. His body although painfully thin was certainly not unpleasant to touch in fact she was sure he had actually gained a little weight in the last couple of weeks, all those scones she thought idly as she allowed her fingers to probe his warm skin.

As Bobby let her fingers roam over his rippling muscles, his own hands were not idle; he began by running his hands up and down Bobby's back and as though by their own volition his fingers found the edge of her cropped blouse, reaching for the soft skin beneath. As his fingers touched Bobby's heated flesh a gasp arose from somewhere and neither knew from who, but it was at this point they both knew what was going to happen next. As Alexander's kisses deepened he began a crab like walk leading them both inside the cottage without their lips separating they managed to end up on the ancient sofa.

Soft murmurings from both, of surprise and pleasure at the surge of feelings they both had for each other, followed with gasps of pure pleasure as they discovered each other in the semidarkness of the old shack. They lay curled together in the aftermath of their love making. Bobby knew that no matter what happened now she was inextricably linked with this wonderful man. She hadn't realised she had been looking… Looking for what? She thought, it was her work, her Magnum Opus. She never in a million years thought it was love.

Tariq and Nazim simply lay outside the door of the cottage waiting patiently for their master to emerge, which he did just before dawn as the sun was just beginning to climb. He left Bobby with a soft kiss and disappeared onto the beach with his faithful companions at his side.

Bobby wondered if it would be awkward seeing Alexander after what had happened the night before. She had never been in a situation like this, she knew that Alexander was vulnerable mentally, but none of his vulnerability had shown in his lovemaking. He had been careful even in the throws of passion, not to allow Bobby's hands to stray towards his injured hip or leg. Bobby felt sure this wasn't because they were painful but that he thought his injuries would in someway be distasteful to her. He couldn't have been more wrong and in time she hoped she could prove this to him.

Bobby took a little more time with her appearance that morning, brushing her newly washed hair until it shone, she wore a pair of pale blue pedal pushers and a little white blouse with the sprigs of green on showed her newly acquired tan off to perfection. The first indication that something wasn't quite as normal was when Bobby noticed the door of the castle was closed and as she looked in the forecourt it was obvious that Alexander's battered old Land Rover was missing.

As Bobby walked a little faster she saw the wooden doors to the go-cart workshop were open and as she got there she saw Tariq and Nazim and knew instantly that Alexander wasn't here. Rory and Mari were putting the finishing touches to their completed go-cart, and were quite obviously bursting with pride to show it off to Bobby. She tried so hard to show her interest and smile her appreciation at their efforts, while inside her heart was sinking from pure disappointment. Why today, thought Bobby, why now?

"Oh Mum says we had to tell you she needed to see you about something when you arrived. Were going to test drive the battler if you'd like to stay you could help us?"

Bobby gave her brightest smile saying she thought she had better go and see what their mother wanted. But, that she would love to see the battler another day, saying quite genuinely what a wonderful job they had made of it and both Uncle Xander and their dad should be very proud of them both.

When Bobby got to the gatehouse she shouted from the back door and entered as she had been told on numerous occasions to do. Morag was baking as usual. On Saturday mornings she baked enough to fill her freezer for the week. This also included not only baking but cooked casseroles, as she had always been a working mum she had learned to be very organised.

Her experience and organisation would be perfect when she opened the tearooms Bobby had no doubt.

"Hi Bobby have a seat." As Bobby sat down she had a terrible feeling that she was going to be told something she wouldn't like, bad news thought Bobby with a sudden feeling of dread.

"Erm I see the Land Rover's not there, is Xander out?"

"Well yes lass, erm he must have got a call early this morning and he left for Glasgow about eight. He left the dogs and asked me to tell you he was sorry he'd been called away. I'm sorry Bobby, this must be so hard for you understand, it's not even easy for us to understand although we have sort of got used to it."

"Oh it's fine, I mean he doesn't have to tell me where he's going after all…"

As Bobby's voice trailed away Morag heard the slight crack.

"I'm sorry Bobby, that he was called away just as he was so happy, and a man on a galloping horse can see how much the two of you care for each other. And why, this morning of all mornings?"

As Morag said this Bobby's face coloured brightly as Morag went on to explain her statement.

"Oh I'm sorry I shouldn't have said anything, I only meant, that well… Err well the dogs weren't outside his door and their were no lights in the castle last night… so I sort of put two and two together as you were both so happy last night after the wonderful news about the bank loan."

As Bobby recovered her surprise and realising it was nothing to feel uncomfortable about, as both Morag and Duncan were as happy as she herself was that she and Alexander were becoming close. They simply wanted Alexander to be happy and she made him happy.

"I realise I have no real right to know Morag, but Xander comes back from Glasgow so depressed. It's as though he has only just emerged from his depression when he gets a phone call and he sinks back. He is so unhappy when he returns, what can make that happen?"

"I wish I knew, all I know for sure is, you, have made him happy, he has almost been like the Alexander I met when I was first dating Duncan. He could be such fun and they were both mad, wild by all accounts, when they were children. He was fantastic with Rory and Mari when they were babies, he's still good with them but, reserved and it's not only his injuries it's more than that, it's as though he is afraid to care or love again… Does that sound strange?"

Instead of feeling angry at Alexander's sudden departure, especially after what they had meant to each other only a matter of hours ago, and after talking to Morag Bobby knew that she must be patient, more patient than she had ever been before if she wanted to understand this complex man.

She decided to keep herself busy, and take this opportunity to take Morag up on her kind offer of the use of her washing machine and wash her meagre collection of clothes which she was fast running out of. All washed and blowing in the wind on Morag's enormous washing line, Bobby went down to the Battlers' shed and sat on the ground where Rory and Mari were putting a final transfer they had found in the tool box onto the Battler, it was from an old bicycle and actually said Raleigh but it looked cool they said and Bobby agreed.

Bobby spent the day just messing around with the children, and then they all walked the dogs on the beach arriving back in time for tea. After the children had gone to bed and the three grown ups were enjoying a glass of wine at the kitchen table which had become the habit lately, Duncan began to reminisce about the happy times he and Alexander had when they were children.

"If anyone had ever told me that Alexander would be the way he is, suffering the way he does, oh I don't mean his leg, I mean his mental demons these fits of depression he gets into, and I would have called them a liar. I would have argued that I knew everything there was to know about my brother, but not the man who came back from Iraq, this man is different, another Alexander, even father wouldn't recognise him."

"He'll come out of it Duncan, you'll see."

Morag said, putting her arm around Duncan's shoulders and giving them a firm squeeze in order to comfort him.

"There's been such a change in him since he's met Bobby and now that we are starting the businesses, he's even stopped sanding the great hall floor until you could see your face in it. Remember when you first came Bobby, that's all he ever did, over and over like a sort of penance. But now it's finished and he's put the armour back on the walls and the grand tapestries. He even finished one of the bedrooms and the next thing is he'll be moving himself back inside instead of living in that outbuilding. He wouldn't even consider living at the gatehouse with us even temporarily, as we said to him on numerous occasions. But I don't think he was ready to be in anyone's company then, but now, oh Duncan now he's so much better."

"That's due to you Bobby, you're like a breath of fresh air, it must be difficult for you to understand… You know his mood swings and disappearances… But please don't let that put you off … Xander is a great guy… And we can tell you like him…?"

They both looked expectantly at Bobby who couldn't help but blush, lowering her eyes as she felt they could see right into her memory of what had passed between Alexander and herself only a matter oh hours ago.

"I do like Xander, very much, and please don't worry on my account, as long as he needs me, then I'll be here."

Chapter 18

Bobby walked up to the castle early on Monday morning not knowing what to expect, so when the first thing she saw was Alexander's Land Rover in the courtyard, standing next to a battered old builder's pickup with the fading name of McKinley on the side, her heart began to pound, in fact she could have sworn it missed a beat, she suddenly felt so overwhelmed that she would see him again she actually felt a little nervous because she hadn't seen him since they had made wonderful, passionate love together in their old shack.

The dogs saw her coming and actually walked away from the

castle door and came towards her in a greeting. Now that's a first thought Bobby, well at least the dogs trust me now. She tentatively called a greeting to the voices inside and was greeted in return as the voices made their way outside.

Alexander looked tired and drawn but a sight for sore eyes as far as Bobby was concerned. He made the introductions as they walked towards the stables, which was the building first on the list. Mr McKinley told Alexander and Bobby that he knew of a good carpenter who was reliable and reasonable who could do the shop fitting much cheaper than any commercial firm.

"Shelves and things for your gift shop and your market garden produce wouldn't be any problem," He explained that you could buy ready made stalls for the toilets that you simply bolted to the floor. Alexander and Duncan intended to do the plumbing but would maybe call on Mr McKinley's expertise if they got stuck they said. To which they had a good laugh, but he agreed he would be onsite for any advice he could give. Mr McKinley left after having a good look around all the chosen buildings with his tattered old notebook he was constantly writing himself little notes and then off he went. It was agreed that work would start first thing in the morning.

As his battered old truck trundled noisily down the gravel path Bobby lifted her eyes to look at Alexander who was closing the double doors of the stables when he caught sight of her intense stare. He looked heartbreakingly handsome but fragile.

Determined not to mention Glasgow at all and to be totally upbeat about the project, Bobby said the first thing that came into her head. "Well, while you have been out on the tiles Alexander Balfour, Morag and I have been planning what kind of décor the tea room is going to have." Suddenly realising what she had said, Bobby could have bitten her tongue off. What on earth made her say that about him being out on the tiles for God's sake?

The sheer look of horror in her eyes must have told Alexander that she realised she had said the wrong thing. Instead of being angry he suddenly felt upset that they couldn't simply have a joke about his disappearance, it wasn't Bobby's fault; none of it was her fault. She was the one good thing in his horizon, and he was determined she shouldn't have the fear he had just seen in her eyes simply for speaking out in jest.

With an enormous effort to shed the usual feelings of depression he always had when coming back from Glasgow, Alexander took up

Bobby's topic about décor of all things.

"Don't tell me the interior's probably going to be something totally outlandish if you two have had your heads together."

Glad that the sticky moment had passed Bobby kept the conversation all in the same light vein. "I missed you!"

I'm sorry I had to go just… When… Well, at that particular moment…" Alexander said this to Bobby as they wandered into Duncan's beautiful peaceful garden where all that could be heard was early morning bird song. They sat down on one of the bench seats where they often sat with Duncan and Morag but now they were alone.

Alexander took hold of one of Bobby's hands and stroked his thumb back and forth, as though thinking of what he wanted to say and how to say it very carefully.

" Look... I'm sorry…"

Bobby suddenly lifted the hand he was holding and gripped his firmly and looked directly into Alexander's face as she said, "Xander, please don't be sorry, don't feel you have to explain anything to me. I realise you have baggage, I cannot begin to understand, but one day when you feel you can let me in on your troubles and thoughts, then I'll be here…. And, as long as you come back… Erm to me… That's if you want me? Then I'll be here for you… ok? Now let's forget it for now and get started on Morag's tea room, because I must tell you she has actually tendered her resignation!!! Yes, there was no stopping her."

Alexander leaned forward slowly letting his lips rest gently on Bobby's soft moist open mouth in a long lingering kiss, before saying, "Whoever the lucky leprechaun was that sat on my shoulder when I placed that add in the paper to hire out my old shack, I hope he finds his pot of gold because I've certainly found mine." Pulling Bobby up and pulling her excitably towards the stables he said, "To work woman, to work."

Chapter 19

It was the last days of June and each of the buildings were now unrecognisable as the unused outbuildings they were less than a month ago. The whole place had been a hive of industry with delivery vans, builder's equipment, cement mixers and the like, all over the gravel path. It looked at one stage worse than it did before they started then suddenly as the builder's equipment began to leave and the forecourt emptied you could begin to see all of the hard work.

All those days when Duncan came straight in from his job as a teacher, only to don his filthy old clothes and join Alexander and Bobby, in being a plumber or a carpenter or a painter or simply a gofer, were beginning to pay off. Morag seemed to spend hours in the kitchen if not cooking for the hungry hordes but filling the freezer full of scones and cakes for 'The Stables' that was how she now thought of it constantly.

Alexander suddenly stood up from the table and announced while they were all sat having dinner that he was declaring a holiday.

"As you all know, tomorrow is the grand go-cart race and The Balfour Battler rides again!"

A massive cheer from Rory and Mari ensued until they were

quietened with a tap on the table with a soupspoon by their uncle in a courtroom Judge style fashion.

"So I propose that Duncan and I take the Battler in the Land Rover and Bobby you go with Morag, Rory and Mari in her car."

"And what do you say we all have a BBQ on the beach, for dinner; win or loose?" said Bobby, determined that tomorrow would be the children's day and she knew how much they wanted a bonfire on the beach. The children were so ecstatic Morag declared they wouldn't sleep a wink all night, but she agreed it would be a wonderful rest from the hard slog of the past few weeks. And a nice rest from cooking just for a change, as the men usually attended to the BBQ she informed Bobby.

It was a beautiful morning as Duncan and Alexander carefully loaded the Battler onto the Land Rover watched by a very nervous Rory and Mari.

"Don't worry we've wedged it in, nothing will happened to it, I promise you." Duncan tried to calm their fears about their precious cargo. Last day of term was a party atmosphere and more so than ever since the introduction of the go-cart idea. There were stalls with orange and lemon squash and home made biscuits for sale to raise funds for some good cause or another.

Bunting was strung up along the starting line and at the bottom of the very steep hill which the go-carts were to descend.

"Oh my, I'm not going to watch, they are bound to tip over or hit something or worse and damage their teeth, oh dear I wish I'd said no in the beginning." Morag was a bag of nerves, while Alexander and Duncan were enjoying the build-up as much as Rory and Mari. They were giving them last minute tips on how to turn and when to apply the brake. Morag had insisted they wear their bicycle helmets or she wouldn't allow them to race, and they had reluctantly agreed, now both had their crash helmets on which only made Morag worse, thinking they were in some sort of high speed motor race instead of a go-cart.

"Listen Morag, why don't you go and sit at that table over there and have yourself a cold drink, I'll watch and cheer them on for you, and don't worry it'll all be over before you know it. And besides Duncan and Xander will be cheering as well, louder than anyone in the crowd I suspect judging by their behaviour, so you don't have to watch."

Morag agreed but reluctantly, she was torn between being a good mother and cheering her children on and worrying herself to death imagining all kinds of terrible injuries which could befall them.

Suddenly Duncan and Alexander were standing with Bobby at the start line with all the other anxious parents, shouting last minute instructions to Rory and Mari who looked really intense. Anyone watching could have been fooled into thinking that the line up of weird and wonderful go-carts were high profile racecars at Brands Hatch.

The flag was raised by a rather jolly plump headmaster, dressed in what he liked to call his holiday informal wear, "Especially for these occasions", he told everyone with a chuckle. He began the count, which seemed to take an inordinately long time and designed to jangle the nerves of the young contestants, never mind the parent drivers who were only spectators. Then suddenly… they were off!!

Down the hill bobbing and weaving all over the track, one or two go-carts tipped over within minutes of setting off, but Rory and Mari leaned into the course like professional racing car drivers while Duncan, Alexander and Bobby were hopping up and down, cheering them on at the top of their voices. Bobby couldn't believe she was almost as bad as Duncan and Alexander, she had no idea what came over her but suddenly more than anything she wanted Rory and Mari to win.

One or two lost wheels and the odd catastrophe before the finish line by some of the go-carts, Bobby, Duncan and Alexander took to their heels and ran down to the finish line just in time to see Rory and Mari cross in first place, hands in the air in true racing driver style, and the three adults yelled in delight.

The presentation for the small but very, very important silver cup followed shortly after and was cheered on in true champion style by all four adults, as by this time Morag was just as thrilled as the others and now it was all over she felt a little foolish to worry about such a small thing she would say dismissively, but glad it was all over just the same.

The triumphant pair didn't want their special racecar to travel in the back of the Land Rover all on its own and so persuaded Morag to let them travel in the back with the car. Morag decided what the heck, she couldn't very well dampen their spirits after all, today was their day, so they travelled back like race car drivers with their vehicle.

Morag and Bobby followed behind with the windows wide open for the heat, cheers and chants could be heard of "We are the Champions, hip, hip hooray." It was a perfect night, the weather was still glorious and after the men had safely put the now very important Balfour Battler away in its garage, the night celebration of a BBQ on the beach could begin.

Duncan and Alexander had obviously built fires on the beach for most of their lives, for within minutes they had piled the driftwood in a heap and surrounded the heap with stones found nearby. The BBQ was an ancient one, kept at the cottage for the fishermen really, but which was regularly cleaned or Morag would not have eaten a morsel cooked on it otherwise she said.

At the beginning of the evening the mood was that of jubilation, as the children recounted their win and others' misfortunes, praise was heaped on the two for their diligence in repairing and restoring the old Battler.

As everyone had eaten their fill from the BBQ and the evening wore on, Duncan and Morag lounged against the old driftwood log where the blanket had once again been laid and piled with cushions from the cottage. Morag lay with Duncan's strong arm around her as they totally relaxed for the first time in what seemed like weeks to both of them. They watched with a knowing smile on their faces as Alexander and Bobby walked hand in hand along the shoreline and listened as Rory and Mari planned another adventure, which of course would include the Battler.

"Can you believe how far we've all come in the last few weeks, especially Xander? You know… everything changed when Bobby came and do you know it would never be the same if she left." Morag spoke quietly in a lethargic thoughtful tone.

"Don't you worry on that score, if I know Xander he won't let this little jewel slip through his fingers. He may be addled at present but he's still a man, and anyone can see he's head over heels in love with the girl. No, he'll not let her go …well unless some catastrophe occurs to blow it. But I tell you this for nothing, if anything happens in an attempt to derail those two from being together, they'll have us to contend with …Eh girl?"

"Too right!" Was Morag's reply.

It was much later when the sky was full of stars and the chill eventually forced the party to break up. An occasional spark still spat from the embers of the campfire as it gradually sank into the sand. Duncan, Morag and the children had a slow walk back towards the gatehouse, leaving Alexander and Bobby to say their goodnights. But tonight Alexander had no intentions of leaving Bobby without first feeling her arms wrap around him the way they had when they had made love for the first time.

Reluctant to leave such a beautiful sky and the last embers of warmth from the campfire, Alexander went into the cottage and returned with one of the duvets which they used to wrap around themselves, taking Duncan and Morag's place against the old log piled with cushions. It was there under the perfect sky of black velvet and silver stars that they made love for the second time, slow, passionate, heart-rending love, without the need for words. Alexander and Bobby knew that there was dozens of questions left unasked, but tonight was not the time. Tariq and Nazim lay like bookends, quiet and loyally,

protecting the lovers from the
outside world, for now.

Chapter 20

The days which followed were non-stop, busy, busy, but happy, oh so happy, Bobby hadn't ever been so happy and she felt sure that went for Alexander too. It was on one of those busy days when Alexander was in the tearoom, finishing last minute jobs and Bobby was helping Duncan and Morag in the gift shop stacking shelves when the crunch of tyres on the gravel told of a visitor.

As they all carried on working assuming whoever it was would give a shout if they needed one of them, it was with a certain amount of surprise when they heard a man's voice shouting.

"Major Balfour, Major Alexander Balfour?"

The whole group suddenly stopped what they were doing and moved automatically towards the open door and into the court yard. Parked in the courtyard, was a smart sleek black motor car, its owner presumably, was the very tall well built formally dressed man, who called for Alexander. Who at that precise moment came out of the tearoom, slightly wary at being called by his Rank rather than his name.

"Yes, that's me, can I help you?"

The two men eyed each other up, the expression on their faces giving nothing away. It was then that the visitor walked towards the rear of his car, pulled open the passenger door and spoke to the passenger who climbed out of the vehicle. It was a girl in her mid twenties, holding a child, who was possibly eighteen months or two years old. They climbed out of the car and looked directly towards Alexander. The child clearly recognised Alexander as he pointed towards him with his podgy little finger.

"I'm returning your responsibility to you!" yelled the man, "I think you owe her something don't you? After all, it's clear that you can afford to pay for your little indiscretion but you leave her to live in a tenement, in the heart of Glasgow."

It was when the stranger said the words Glasgow that Bobby took a sharp intake of breath. Thinking she was about to faint she began hyperventilating and repeating the words, "No, no, no," and between each cry huge sobs involuntarily began to escape from her throat.

Hardly aware of what she was doing she dropped the ball of twine she had in her hand and suddenly began to run – run towards the sanctuary of the beach. Her mind was racing, telling herself he had a child, that's why he kept going to Glasgow. That's why, she told herself, why he felt guilty when he came back, because he knew this lady was left behind in some tenement building. That's why he felt guilty about living in the castle.

Without knowing exactly what she was doing Bobby began to stuff her meagre belongings into her holdall, she collected her lap top and started to push everything into her ancient car. Jumping into the car Bobby started the engine of her battered old Citroen and gave silent thanks that it hadn't chosen this time to break down. She revved the engine and began to reverse the car out of the hole to which it had sank, as the car began to heave itself out of the sand which held it like tooth being pulled from its socket it suddenly jumped back and roared in it's retreat.

All the time Bobby had been packing and speeding her way home she would never know how long the tears continued to roll down her cheeks. She drove and drove having no idea how she got there, she eventually arrived back to the relative safety of her old station house.

She pushed open the living room door exhausted and for the moment she thought she couldn't cry another tear, when two pairs of eyes looked up from the sofa where they had been quietly watching a movie, in absolute shock and amazement.

"Bobby, what the..?"

Bobby burst into the most heart wrenching sobs she hadn't known she could produce. The two girls jumped up, reaching for her before she collapsed into their arms as her knees simply gave way underneath her. They sat her down on the sofa, Suze went for a bottle of wine, while Penny turned the TV off, it was obvious to all three girls that no one would sleep tonight, as she explained what had happened to cause this sudden return, when the last they had heard was that she was ecstatically happy.

Bobby started slowly; she told them how Alexander had been in Iraq and suffered terrible injuries, which not only affected his body but also his mental health. She explained how she felt she had begun to breakdown the barriers between the past and a possible future. They knew of course about the restoration of the castle but also the alterations to the outbuildings into new and viable businesses.

Bobby told of how Duncan and Morag were thrilled at the change which she seemed to have brought about in Alexander's demeanour, he had less mood swings, he seemed to have lost that compulsive obsessive behaviour which he had displayed when he had first come back from The Queen Elizabeth Hospital in Birmingham where he had been evacuated to and where he had done his recuperation.

Bobby knew she was gabbling but couldn't stop herself, it was as though she were telling herself how she thought she had changed his life, how she thought he wanted her, needed her, had made love to her. "When all the time he had a… girlfriend? And a….baby in Glasgow." All the time she said, when he had disappeared to Glasgow, and she didn't know why, she just knew he was depressed and back to square one when he came home. His family, wonderful family, all felt as though they had to walk on eggshells when he came back from one of his disappearing acts when all the time he was going to see his other woman and baby! She sobbed again, a deep heart-wrenching sob as she said to the girls who had listen in silence.

"But.. I love him… I can't help it, I know I'm a fool but I love him… if he had only told me! Explained to me… I love him Suze.. Penny… I love him…what am I going to do, how will I go on without him?"

And she dissolved into floods of uncontrollable tears which all they could was make the soothing sounds of comfort until the flood subsided. They helped her up to her old room and into bed reminding her that if she needed anything at all she simply had to call.

Chapter 21

Bobby wasn't to know what had happened after hearing those words, words she would never forget. "I'm returning your responsibility to you." Alexander had been momentarily dumb struck at seeing Cindy and young Archie with this man, who seemed to be blaming him for something.

Alexander's brain had been trained professionally to deal with unusual situations while thinking on his feet, he calculated that the man thought he had abdicated his responsibility in someway for Cindy and Archie's care, so he asked himself, was it her brother, another relative? There had to be a connection that would explain the man's apparent anger with him.

"I am Major Balfour and who may I ask, are you? Before, we get into the specifics about my responsibility towards Cindy and Archie."

"I am Jonathan McDonald."

This was said as though Alexander should know who he was, however the name completely escaped him for the moment, until Cindy enlightened him by informing the listening group who stood silently in shock.

"This is my Brother in-law Alexander, Archie's brother from

Edinburgh. And I'm so sorry about this, I am so embarrassed, I tried to explain to him, how good you've been to me and Archie."

"I'll bet he's been good to you, he can afford to be good to you, he is obviously a very wealthy man yet he leaves you to bring up his child in a tenement building when he lives in a castle."

"Stop, stop it, stop it, I keep telling you the wean is Archie's not Alexander's. Alexander was Archie's Commanding Officer. He has been wonderful to wee Archie and me, I don't know how I would have coped without his help. Tell him, Alexander, tell him please, he won't believe me and he bullied me into coming here. He thinks that I'm a Glasgow slut who would sleep with another man while my husband was fighting for his country in Iraq. He thinks because I come from Glasgow that I'm not good enough for his family, that's why Archie and I had to run away to get wed before he went overseas, because his family wouldn't agree. They said I was just a crush and he would soon get over me. They wanted him to go into the army and see the world, I just wanted him to be my husband and a father to our child."

"Well she's loyal to you Balfour, I'll say that for her, but I saw the evidence with my own eyes, there is a framed photograph of you and young Archie sitting on her sideboard. Why would she have a photo of you sitting on her sideboard and not one of her dead husband?"

"Because I can't bear to see his face, can't bear for my child to see the man he'll never call daddy, I have Alexander's photo so that wee Archie knows what it's like to have a man in his young life."

As she said this, the girl who looked pale, drawn and desperately underweight, drew out of her bag a sheaf of papers and a plastic holder with two photographs safely tucked inside. She handed the baby to Alexander who took the willing child as he had quite obviously held him on numerous occasions as anyone could see from the ease with which he held the child.

The girl took the small plastic folder which held two photographs inside and handed them to her brother in-law. On one side was a photograph of a couple, quite obviously happy, one of them was his younger brother Archie and the other was Cindy, they were quite clearly, for all the world to see very much in love. Cindy explained it was taken on their wedding day when they ran away to Gretna Green to be married before he shipped out to Iraq.

"You can see the lucky heather we both had as our button holes, there wasn't time to get anything else and it didn't really matter, being together, getting married was all that mattered to Archie and me."

The other photo was of a beaming Archie taken in his uniform holding his new baby son, facing him towards the camera as any proud father would be, showing off his first born son to the world. There was a stunned silence; you could have heard a pin drop except for the chattering baby who was in the process of poking his podgy finger into Alexander's mouth so that he would pretend to bite it off as he normally did when he played with him.

"I also have my marriage certificate and Archie's birth certificate if you care to look at them."

"Why, why didn't you tell us, you had a child, why didn't you let us know that my parents had a grandchild?" pleaded Jonathan. "They had a right to know. And why does *he* come and visit you in your flat, I've seen him with my own eyes, and you have a photograph of him with the child."

"I'll tell you why, why I never told you about wee Archie, because just as you are doing now you are trying to take over, maybe take my child away from me, say I'm not a fit mother just because I come from the wrong place! Glasgow, not

Edinburgh as you do. We knew
Archie and me that you didn't
approve of me, he told me what
your parents said when he said he
wanted to marry me, they thought I
was common.

"But we loved each other, and he
was sure they would eventually
come round to liking me when they
got to know me. But we never got
the chance, when I fell pregnant and
I knew Archie would be in Iraq, I
didn't want his parents to know, I
wanted him with me when we told
them. The only reason Archie got to
see the baby when he was born was
because Alexander, Major Balfour,
gave him four days leave. He broke
all the rules to allow it, other
soldier's wives had had babies and

their husbands had not been allowed to go home. But… it was as though the Gods knew that Archie would never come back to me again."

"So why, why didn't you tell us about the child after Archie died. Didn't you think we had a right to know?"

"I'll tell you why, because at the funeral, which if the army hadn't released Archie's body to my care, you and your family would have taken over completely. You knew I was Archie's lawful wedded wife or the MOD would not have released his body to me, and yet you all completely ignored me, I've never felt so utterly alone and wretched in my life and hope I never have to again. You all knew about our marriage, I know you did because he told me he had written to everyone explaining all about our wedding at Gretna Green. He said he was sorry to have to do it that way but he hoped you would all understand in time. I know he told you all he loved me as I did him more than anything in the world. Yet you totally ignored me, you froze me out when I needed you most and you ask me why?"

"But that doesn't answer why Major Balfour is so involved with you and the child, unless he comes to 'comfort you'."

If Alexander hadn't been holding Archie he would have knocked the head off Jonathan who spat out his hateful accusation. Alexander handed Archie back to Cindy and stood so close to his accuser but instead of denying his accusations and standing up for himself he declared,

"The reason I look out for Cindy and Archie are not for the reason you imagine but because it was my fault that Archie died!!!

"Alexander!" Was exclaimed by all three bystanders who knew that, such a thing could never be true."

"If I hadn't been *busy*, called to a meeting, Archie might have still been here." Alexander ground the words out as though they pained him to speak aloud. "I would have been leading that patrol; it was my job, my responsibility to bring those young men home safely, me that should have been killed instead of Archie."

The silence that fell over the small group, all standing motionless in the middle of the courtyard was eerily calm after the heated words of minutes ago. Until Morag bravely cleared her throat and spoke up; "This is no place to be discussing such things and surely you would like to sit down Cindy, Archie must be very heavy, at least please come and sit in the tea room and talk like civilised people."

At first she though they were going to ignore her request but as Cindy made towards a table and chairs so that she could sit Archie down the others followed her inside. Cindy went to Alexander and placed her hand on his arm.

"Alexander, it was not your fault, it wasn't anyone's fault, you couldn't have known. Even the MOD letter told me that, he led his men bravely and died doing the job he loved. You have to stop punishing yourself and I have to stop relying on you. It's just sometimes,…..I miss him so much and I don't know which way to turn."

Cindy gulped back a tear as Morag went to sit next to her and put a comforting arm around her shoulder.

"I would just like to know one more thing," stated a still puzzled Jonathan, "before we leave. Where were you Major, on the day of my brother's funeral? His Captain was there, his comrades were there but where were you?"

"I can answer that Mr McDonald!"

Alexander tried to stop Duncan, saying it didn't matter anymore, but Duncan would not be stopped. He was like a lion protecting his cub, now that it had become clear that far from having an affair with the widow of one of his soldiers he was in fact supporting her as he knew he would be, there was no way Jonathan was going to get away with accusing Alexander of not caring enough to be at one of his men's funeral.

"My brother was not at the funeral of your brother, because he was in The Queen Elizabeth Hospital in Birmingham fighting for his own life."

Cindy spoke up saying, "Alexander wasn't even aware of the funeral or anything else until I wrote to him. I read about his injuries in the newsletter that is sent to the wives and mothers of army personnel. I'm ashamed to say I sent him my address and asked him to come. I needed to know why. Why had Archie gone out and led a patrol? He was just a boy…. I wanted someone to blame, I wanted to blame Alexander. I realise now that by ringing him whenever I needed him I was feeding a need to keep Archie alive and at the same time I was hurting Alexander. I needed him yet I needed someone to blame too.

"I'm ashamed of myself Alexander, you have been the kindest person and it was wrong of me to hold on to you, not giving you time to come to terms with your own demons which were obvious for all to see. Yet… just recently you seem different, there has been something about you, a change has come over you.. And I'm glad for you though I was jealous at first. It was obvious you had met someone and I thought it was unfair that you could begin your life again, while I would never be able to do that. I would be forever alone without the man I loved. But I was wrong, Alexander, wrong to begrudge you happiness when you'd done so much for Archie and me, when no one else cared. From now on I hope we can simply be friends, people who once knew a great guy, a great soldier and a wonderful husband. But no more than that, I want to rebuild my life, it's time, don't you think?"

"If you're sure Cindy, I'll always be here no matter what other people think. You can always count on me."

Jonathan McDonald stood up. "From now on Major Balfour, Cindy will not be alone." As he said this he moved closer to Cindy and Archie, placing a protective arm around them.

"She will have a family. She is part of the McDonald family and we take care of our own."

Jonathan looked directly into Alexander's face, his eyes glared as Alexander said, "She didn't appear to have a family before so what guarantee do you give she will be cared for now?"

"My word Major Balfour, you have my word that Cindy and the child… my nephew will receive the best of care."

Alexander saw a flicker of what looked like discomfort in his opponent's eyes, at what had gone before in the McDonald family.

Certainly they had not covered themselves in glory thought Jonathan and would need to go a long way to gain his sister in-law's trust and that of the child. But his parents would be thrilled to have a grandchild, Archie's child – oh what a day that will be when they meet their son's child for the first time.

As the small entourage got back into the car, this time in very different circumstances, Alexander reminded Cindy that she could still always come to him for help if the need arose. Alexander squeezed Cindy's hand in an effort to let her know that life would be better for them all from this day, he felt sure of that. He ruffled the now sleeping Archie's hair and touched his podgy little hand in farewell.

Jonathan McDonald surprised the group by shaking Alexander's hand saying he was sorry for any misunderstanding and not to worry about Cindy he would take good care of both her and Archie. And with that, the long sleek car pulled away in a crunch of gravel, just as it had arrived.

Chapter 22

Bobby sat curled up in the ancient armchair of her aunt's, by her bedroom window. A slight breeze fluttered past her tear-swollen face as she stared fixedly out onto the empty street that would before long have the usual early risers of Hollybush going about their business.

Upon a knock at the station house door, Penny arose. She was in the middle of her hurried toast and coffee, before dashing to open the gift shop after sleeping later than normal due to the traumatic events of the night before. Pulling open the door she took a step back as standing in the doorway was a man so tall he almost blocked out the morning sunlight.

"I don't need three guesses to know who you are," Penny almost spat the words out.

"Please before you go any further, or slam the door in my face, I can explain but I would much rather explain to Bobby. But please, please believe me when I tell you it's not how it looked and I need to be able to see her to explain it in person."

By this time Suze was standing next to Penny as their eyes took in this gorgeous looking guy, who looked like a younger version of Rambo, in his attire of bottle green army t-shirt that showed off every muscle to perfection both girls thought simultaneously. As their eyes travelled downward they saw the army fatigues which was his standard dress and which hung onto his lean hips.

"Yup this is definitely Alexander!"

The two girls looked at each other their eyebrows lifting at the situation they had here. Their friend was upstairs desperately unhappy without this gorgeous chunk of manhood and he was down here desperate to make things right, and their dilemma was? They both thought again in unison.

"No contest!" They said together. "Up the stairs, first door on your right, and you had better be telling it straight or we'll be back!" The two girls said in a terrible imitation of Arnold Schwarzenegger, and rolled their eyes at their own bad joke.

"We have to go to work now, but we are only just across the yard, if you need us!"

Alexander thanked the girls profusely, promising Bobby wouldn't need reinforcements. The two girls departed still eating their toast but managed to chat almost in unison at the rate of knots.

Bobby had heard the front door slam and presumed that one of the girls had gone out to work when she heard a light tap on her bedroom door.

"It's open."

As the door opened Bobby turned slightly to see who it was, she had never been so surprised as she was when standing there, half hidden by the door was a heart wrenching gorgeous looking Alexander. Bobby who had been sat in the chair all night and who had on nothing more than her skimpy shorts and vest top which were standard nightwear nowadays, suddenly felt very naked. She was about to stand up and fuss about getting a dressing gown, anything to put off what he was going to say, what she was about to hear, that she didn't want to hear.

When he spoke first, his voice was unlike the voice she was used to, the quiet but firm Xander. This was a nervous, unsure of himself Alexander, who stumbled over his words in an effort to be heard before he thought she would throw him out.

"Bobby, I need you to hear me out before you throw me out, please. Will you let me tell you about Cindy and Archie and Glasgow before you jump to any conclusions? But the first thing I must tell you before I go any further, is that Archie, wonderful though the wee boy maybe is not my son, and I am not having and never have had an affair with Cindy!!"

Bobby suddenly launched herself up from her seat and into Alexander's wonderful arms, kissing his wonderful face, his eyes, his, cheeks.

"Oh Xander I'm so sorry, I have sat here all night thinking what a fool I have been, running away like that, not even giving you a chance to explain. I'm so, so sorry, I judged you, yet I knew inside that the person that man was talking about wasn't capable of getting a girl pregnant then leaving her to bring up a child on her own. I'm so ashamed; I need you to forgive me."

Alexander hushed her protests by putting his lips firmly on hers with a kiss so deep, a kiss he thought he would never have another chance to do again after she ran away.

"You have nothing to be ashamed of, in fact you have shown more patience and understanding than any of the councillors the army sent me to see. I'm sorry that I didn't explain about Cindy and Archie. Whenever things got too much for Cindy and she needed support I told her she could ring me and I would be there for her.

"Each time I came back from Glasgow with the intention of telling you, the feelings of guilt at leaving Cindy and Archie in that god awful flat made me so depressed. There was I was coming home to a life of luxury in comparison to what poor Cindy had. And the more my life seemed to be improving all I could think about was that it was my fault.

"I'm not making any sense I know, but I need to explain some of what happened in order to make some sort of sense of it myself."

Bobby took hold of Alexander's hand and led him towards the two ancient armchairs where she had been sat when he arrived. As he sat down she could tell it was difficult for him as he rubbed his hands together in an effort to find a place to begin his story.

"You see, Archie, that's young Archie's dad, he shouldn't have been taking a patrol out, he was just a boy. It should have been me, it should have been me." Alexander repeated in a tormented voice.

"I'll never forget …….. a few days before the patrol we had been marching through the town and an old man, a village elder apparently…a hundred years old they said, he came up to me as we passed through the village and he put his hand on my arm as I stood aside while the men marched through. He said in his broken English, how pleased he was, how happy he was that we had come to protect his people, and his smile, I'll never forget that toothless smile, as I thanked him and walked on with my men.

"A few days later as I was about to take my platoon on patrol I received a call, an urgent call it said to a meeting with local official's and town elders. There was trouble of some sort brewing and they needed a show of top brass and I was it. There was a chain of command of course so the patrol would be fully manned and strictly speaking I wouldn't be missed although I much preferred to take my own patrols out.

"As I arrived a the perimeter border control sheds where the meeting was to be held, I saw what looked like the elderly man who had approached me in the street a few days earlier. His face was pressed against the wall and his arm was behind him as he was forcibly being searched by a young MP, before entering the meeting. The elderly man looked up and saw me, he saw that I recognised him, but the look in his eyes was not the kindly look of the old gentleman who had previously thanked us for coming to save his people. The look in his face was of fear, and distrust, and a terrible sadness which I shared as I looked into his craggy old face.

"I have asked my self many times, was the young MP wrong in what he did? Was he not simply carrying out the training which he had been taught to follow as his life could depend upon it? Or could he have dealt differently with the elderly gentleman? Could he have been more respectful in his search? However knowing what I now know of insurgents who strap bombs and explosives under their flowing gowns, was he simply being diligent in his search?

"Anyway the meeting was the usual chaotic shouting match between two cultures and many different dialects with only one interpreter. I returned to the barracks, it was just in time to see the helicopter flying

in the wounded and… the dead…
Archie was the soldier who had
died blown up by an IED…"

Bobby wanted to reach out and hold
him but she knew this was his time,
it was now or never, the flood gates
had opened and he needed to
unburden himself, so she sat quietly
and listened as he carried on with
his harrowing tale.

"The report which was filed by the
Captain who was on patrol with
Archie said that the IED had been
hidden in the carcase of a dead dog,
which apparently Archie had tried
to move out of his path with the end
of his rifle. So you see it should
have and would have been me, had
I not been called away. It was my

fault that that young man did not get to go home to his young wife and child…

"Then, as though as a sort of retribution within days of Archie dying, I myself was injured by an IED. I knew nothing for months; I was in and out of surgery and spent a very long year at the QE in Birmingham. It wasn't until I received a letter from Cindy asking for my help that I met her and her baby.

"The guilt I feel is not only for Cindy Archie and their wonderful little boy, I feel guilty because I grew up my whole life with no other thought in my head than becoming a soldier. I chose my degree with the soul purpose of its suitability towards my eventual officer training at Sandhurst. I took IT, Physics and Maths all with intention of entering the intelligence corp.

"I chose this, me myself, all I could think about was going to fight. And when the call came and I had finished all my training and was now, Major Alexander Balfour of the Royal Highland Regiment preparing to be shipped to Iraq, all I could think of was how proud my father and grandfather would be of me.

"I was being sent to bring down a dictator, the great and powerful Saddam Hussein and his evil army, to fight for justice, and the safety and freedom for the people of Iraq… Wrong, wrong, wrong. We were pawns in a terrible game; we thought we were fighting to stop the expansion of terrorism.

"But in reality it was more to do with, big money, personal and party ambitions, corporatism. Iraq turned ordinary soldiers into torturers of prisoners and we lost our moral bearings. The war was immoral; we had no right to go interfering in a country's civil unrest. The war between the Sunni and the Shias has gone on for hundreds of years and will go on long after we are all dead. We call those who would protect their lands insurgents or rebels, but wouldn't we do the same, isn't every soldier who joins the army under the impression that's what it's all about? Protecting their country, that's what I believed… how wrong I was.

"All, Father ever wanted was for one of his sons to take over Balfour Castle and yet all I ever wanted to do was to go into the army and Duncan never wanted to inherit the burden. My ambition now is to restore Father's dream and wipe out the past, forget I ever went into the army, I only wish I could tell him. I wished he could have known that it wasn't going to be left to wreck and ruin while I was off fighting in some foreign field.

"I will never fight again and if I have a child I hope that I can explain, explain that there has to be a better way to solve global problems than blowing each other up."

Suddenly there was silence as though Alexander had simply ran out of steam, his head hung low and as he raised his face Bobby could see the tears which had flowed down his cheeks unheeded, he looked empty and devoid of emotion. But there was something else thought Bobby, he looked as though he had shed a great burden which had weighed him down for so long, and it had taken over the real Alexander. The Alexander who

Duncan and Morag remembered, the real Alexander, but each time traces of him began to emerge he was pulled back in the shape of his guilt for the soldier who he believed died in his place. His penance, his self imposed purgatory was to accept Cindy and Archie as constant reminders, of the pain he had inflicted.

Chapter 23

"The man who brought Cindy and Archie to the house was her brother in-law, he thought…. Well you know what he thought, but it's not true, never, ever. I was there to comfort Cindy to help her financially and to be honest I think she wanted me to suffer because Archie had died. We've talked and she realises that it's time, time for us all to move on. She'll never forget Archie and neither will I, but it's time to start over and put the past behind us. Her Brother in-law, despite what you saw and heard actually wasn't a bad chap once he understood the truth. I would hazard a guess that wee Archie will be spoiled from now on when the grandparents find out they have a grandchild .... Archie's son, I also have a feeling they will welcome Cindy into the family, the only thing I wish it could have happened before Archie died.

"So have I blown my chance with you? Or will you still come and help us all put Balfour Castle back on the map?"

Bobby got out of her chair and went to sit on Alexander's knee, then realised she would probably be too heavy for his injured leg so she pulled him up and walked him over towards the double bed before putting both her hands up to his face and drawing him down so that she could kiss him. She kissed his face then his neck and her hands began to move downward towards the bottom of his t-shirt, sliding her warm hands underneath where her fingers instantly came into contact with his taut torso muscles and his sharp intake of breath told her she was having the desired affect.

In an instant Alexander lifted Bobby off her feet and unceremoniously dumped her into the centre of the bed before pulling of his t-shirt and dropping his fatigues where he stood.
As they made love slowly and passionately, with honesty and holding nothing back they both knew that this partnership was not temporary, this was forever. This

was a connection made in heaven and wouldn't be easily broken.

As they lay in each other's arms panting at the sheer exertion of their lovemaking, Bobby joked that he didn't do so bad for an old injured guy. Bobby knew what she was doing, it wasn't a thought that had just popped out of her mouth as her usual clangers did, this was something that also needed to be out in the open so that they could move on and not be embarrassed about it and it wouldn't become an elephant in the corner type of unspoken problem.

"Xander? Do you mind me talking about your leg?"

"I don't mind, but I'm terrified that it will make you sick or disgust you, it's not pretty and I have got used to it where as you have never seen a battle scar before."

"Alexander, I'm not saying it wouldn't upset me, anything that's happened to hurt you would upset me, but if I had been with you if I had been your girlfriend or lover during the time you spent in hospital, I would have already seen the damage. So I would rather we had no secrets, from now on I want us to trust each other and tell each other everything."

"Everything? Are you sure..... Duncan and I were pretty bad when we were young," Joked Alexander.

"You know what I mean…"

Alexander knew exactly what she meant and had simply been trying to inject a little humour into what was sure to be a pretty fraught experience. He threw back the light sheet which was at present covering them and climbed out of bed turning so that Bobby could be in no doubt about what she was letting herself in for, if she took on what was left of his once perfect body.

Bobby looked from his handsome face where he looked directly ahead, holding his breath until the inspection was completed. She looked at his tanned torso, his six-pack stomach which would be the envy of most normal men, and which tapered down to his slender waist to an obvious line where his tan stopped, she looked at his firm white buttocks and then down to the hip and the leg which looked as though some giant monster had taken a huge bite out of him.

The surgeon who had battled to save both the hip and leg with hardly an ounce of flesh to work with should, in Bobby's opinion, be given a medal. The injury had had time to heal and made some attempt at reshaping itself into something that resembled a thigh and a hip and if that was as bad as it got and Alexander had been lucky enough to still have all of his limbs then it was something to celebrate, which was more than some young men could.

Bobby got out of bed and placed her naked body against his, and whispered against his lips.

"Alexander Balfour, I love each and every part of you and your gorgeous body and I thank God for the surgeon who managed to save your leg and your hip for you… not for me"

This time when they made love it was without the aid of a sheet discreetly placed over Alexander's leg, from now on there would be no need to hide or cover his leg ever again. Bobby's suddenly said while trailing her fingers idly over Alexander's heated body.

"From now on I would like you to wear either nothing, or shorts!!!, I don't mind, but I would like you to tan your white bits, when we are back at the beach."

"You're on, now that I know it won't scare you off, Duncan has seen it but Morag and the kids haven't."

"Alexander, you have a wonderful family Morag would want to mother you and the kids will probably think it's cool. And it will be a lot cooler for you in this heat so that's that OK? Now let's go down stairs and have some coffee

I'm suddenly starved. We could go to Suze's tea room but we would have to put some clothes on first… nah… we'll just stay here."

As they went down stairs, Bobby had redressed in her very revealing shorts and top and Xander had actually stopped to put his boxers on which was just as well, as there was the sound of a door opening then in walked a huge bunch of flowers, behind which stood a pair of legs in a pair of tan coloured trousers. It was just then in an instant that Bobby had an inkling of who was behind the flowers and immediately jumped behind Alexander to hide her skimpy outfit. So, there they were, Alexander was standing in his boxer shorts with a kettle in his hand, while Bobby was standing behind him with her arms round his midriff and out popped Kevin from behind the bunch of flowers.

"Surprise! I thought that was your car so I thought I'd just call and see you on the off chance."

It was hard to say who got the biggest surprise, Kevin who couldn't believe his eyes, when he came face to face with an almost naked man with a body like a God, Alexander, who instantly knew that this little wimp was creepy Kevin, or Bobby herself, who was half naked and hidden behind Alexander and nothing to cover herself in order to make her escape without Kevin getting an eye full.

Alexander was amazing. He simply walked both his and Bobby's attached body forward, opening the door for Kevin to exit saying, "It was nice of you to call but the next time you call to see my fiancée could you knock, I'm afraid we didn't hear you this time."

And with that Kevin was on the other side of the door still holding his bunch of rather gaudy flowers. Alexander and Bobby hugged each other laughing at poor Kevin's expression as he had been firmly pushed out the door.

"Are you? Are you my fiancée? Now that you know all my grotty secrets, do you still love me?"

"I would love to be your fiancée, and I'm sure there is still lots of things I still don't know about you, but don't worry I'll ask Duncan and Morag."

"But do you love me?"

"I love you more than I ever thought possible to love anyone and I never even knew I was looking."

"As much as I would love to stay in bed with you all day, I would like you to meet the closest thing I have to family, Suze and Penny who didn't know what had hit them last night when I burst in on them and cried on their shoulders until they must have been fed up to the back teeth of the very mention of Alexander Balfour, so I must put that right in case they also see your Land Rover and come and give you a pasting."

"Too late, I met them this morning, I managed to get one sentence in before they verbally attacked me in your defence, but I would love to meet them under more pleasant circumstances so reluctantly we had better get dressed. Although I wonder, does this little cottage have a shower?"

"Yeess… Nothing fancy but yes."

"Would that shower be big enough for two people?"

"Well I can't say I've ever tried it, but there's only one way to find out!"

Chapter 24

It was over an hour later before two freshly showered bodies made their way towards The Carriages. Bobby texted Penny to ask if she could get someone to cover for her for a little while, and for her to meet her and Alexander at Suze's. As Alexander and Bobby stepped into the wonderful old train, which was now The Carriages tearooms, Alexander was absolutely amazed and totally impressed with what Suze had done with it, giving the tea room the real atmosphere of travelling in a train while having afternoon tea. Right down to the old-fashioned suitcases placed on the luggage rack, it was all wonderful, he said as he shook Suze's hand.

"I love it, you have amazing insight and I can see now what Bobby saw in our old outbuildings."

"Suze, this is Alexander Balfour. I gather you met him briefly this morning? Alexander this is one of my best friends Suze."

As they shook hands Alexander seemed so at ease he actually looked a different guy, so happy and relaxed, even Bobby hadn't seen this side of him the social interactive side, apart from with his own family of course.

Penny arrived minutes later and Alexander being a gentleman, stood up shook her hand, saying he hoped they had both forgiven his rather unorthodox entrance this morning. His arm firmly around Bobby's waist until all four of them sat down in one of the trains booths to have tea and scones.

After all the explanations about the misunderstanding of the previous night were made, Alexander looked at Bobby who could see the look in his eye, and the raise of his eyebrows and understood what he wanted, and she nodded her agreement.

"I hope you will be as happy as Bobby and I are, when I tell you she has agreed to become my fiancée."

"Oh! Congratulations to both of you, how wonderful"

There were kisses all round stretching over the tea table as they hugged each other.

"Oh my goodness won't Kevin be disappointed, he's been watching the cottage for the last two months for any chink of light from your bedroom curtains, signalling you were home. We've run out of ideas to put him off, he tried telling us that the bank needed to talk to you so he must have a number or an address where you could be contacted. But we simply said we didn't know that you had been soooo upset at something, which had happened you had simply dropped off the face of the earth, hah."

"I met Kevin this morning." Alexander said.

" Oh you should have been there, girls it was really funny, Xander was standing in his boxers and I was in my skimmpies and who should come creeping in without so much as a knock, with a huge bunch of those gaudy flowers he brings from the garage in front of his face. Well you should have seen the expression on Kevin's face when Xander, standing directly infront of him, almost naked, thwarted his 'surprise'. It was a scream, and then Xander guided him outside and told him to knock next time he called –

somehow I don't think he'll call again, ha ha ha!"

Both girls looked at each other and simultaneously imagined Alexander standing there with only his boxers on saying, "Wow… we wish we had been there to see that…"

The inference was very obvious and all three girls fell about giggling, however Alexander hadn't a clue what they were laughing about.

"Listen I would like to show Xander the gift shop while we are here then we're going to get going but I want to ask you both a favour. Well we think the grand opening of the tearooms, market garden produce shop and the gift shop will probably be next weekend if we can get everything sorted by then. But I wondered if you could get anyone to cover for you and both of you come up for the big day… and listen you get to sleep in a castle… But before you get too excited you have to bring your own camp bed and sleeping bag as there are no finished bedrooms yet are there Xander although we are making progress."

"Listen to her, would we !!!! I mean, would we miss the chance to sleep in a castle?? And would we miss your grand opening? I mean is the Pope Catholic? Don't worry about us finding someone to cover for us, do you know since we opened the businesses we could employ extra staff on a daily basis we are so busy. Do you know Bobby if creepy Kevin says anything else about the loan Penny and I have decided we are simply going to pay it off… Honestly we have been making incredible profits it won't be a problem ridding ourselves of the little creep."

"Listen you must do whatever you think, but please don't worry on my account, I am not even thinking about the loan the mortgage is being paid and you never know you may want to keep that money to expand… maybe buy the station house from me???"

"You mean you would sell it to us? Would you really Bobby? Does that mean it's the end for the romantic novels then? No more writing for you?"

"Never say never, I may have something different in mind, and as for the house, I think you will have more need for it than me in the future don't you?"

Alexander smiled. "As Bobby has agreed to be my wife, and unless she wants to hang onto the house for another reason, I'm hoping she will share my castle with me!!"

"Oh wow listen to that Penny… 'Share my castle with me,' Oh my God, we're more likely to find someone like creepy Kevin to share our lives with."

"Rubbish, rubbish you are now women of substance and before long you will be able to pick and choose who you want to marry girls!!!!"

As the happy group stood to leave, hugs and kisses were again distributed, Alexander took Bobby by the hand and they made their way to the house to collect her few belongings. As she was packing her few possessions she could hear Alexander on the phone, in a jubilant mood, saying to whoever it was on the other end of the phone, and shouting up the stairs.

"Tell them you are coming home with me!!"

"Who is it, of course I'm coming if you come and give me a hand with these bags there too heavy for me."

He was laughing as he hurried up the stairs to carry both bags, saying, "It was Morag and Duncan and the kids, they were all shouting, they said I had better be bringing you, and not to come back without you and I was promising that I wouldn't."

"You should have been there for my lecture from both Morag and Duncan when they said if I let you go, I must be mentally affected... I mean that's a bit near the mark isn't it?"

Laughing at his own joke as he piled Bobby's things in the Land Rover they walked hand in hand over to the gift shop to take a quick look at what Penny had done with it and pinch some of her ideas for theirs. Bobby told Penny she would leave her battered old Citroen for her and Suze to use and they could drive up in it when she confirmed the grand opening date to them. Another goodbye and a wave to both Penny outside the gift shop and Suze through the little window of her stranded train and off they went.

"Are you happy Bobby? Or are you a little sad at leaving your friends, after all you have been together a very long time."

"I can't deny I love them both, they are like sisters, but I'm not far away, not so far that I couldn't come for the day if I want to and they can do the same. I could never be sorry for how it's turned out for me, how could I be I love you and I couldn't wish for anything else. Although..."

"Although what Bobby tell me, no secrets remember tell me and if it can be done then we'll do it."

Bobby gave a little cough and a slight intake of breath before starting, "Well, emm… Xander I want to ask you something, but I want you to feel free to say no, really I mean that if you don't want to do it then I won't be offended so please feel free."

"I get it, I get it, now get on with it for goodness sake you're making me nervous."

"Ok, well, you know that I came up to the cottage to write and not a romantic novel, I wanted to write something, meaningful, something that I could be proud of and that would actually make a difference… Well, what would you say if in collaboration with you, I wrote a book about the human cost of sending soldiers to war, you know a war in which young men have no idea what the reality is before they go, and can't talk about when they return. About issues such as Post

Traumatic Stress Disorder, about the trauma it causes not only the soldiers but their families too… what do you think?"

Their was a brief silence and Bobby held her breath, wondering if she had rushed it, should she have waited, he had only just come to grips with some of his demons, and now she was expecting him to face them all and not only that, but put it in a book to tell the world. It seemed an age before Alexander pulled the Land Rover into a lay-by and turned towards Bobby with a look of such tenderness in his eyes, he reached towards her pulling her close and placed the tenderest and gentle kiss onto her lips.

"I not only found a pot of gold the day I advertised for someone to hire my shack, I found a jewel. I think that is a wonderful idea, and I agree completely that the horrors of war should be told and so should their affects on each and everyone concerned, wives, mothers, brothers and I know you are the one to tell such a story with truth, sympathy and understanding.

I never ever want to see another war again as long as I live. And part of me wishes I had never gone into the army, yet another part of me knows that I grew up during that time, I saw and did things I never thought I was capable of, so yes I grew as a person but I'm not so sure I grew as a human being, it will take me a very long time to know the answer to that, and if you writing a book which will help others then I will help in anyway I can."

"Then that's all I need to know."

Bobby folded Alexander's hand in hers, then lifted it to her lips and kissed it tenderly.

"Are you happy Xander?"

"Happier than I ever dreamed I could ever be, and for the first time in a very long time, I don't feel the slightest guilt that I can feel this much happiness, and I owe it all to you my darling."

Chapter 25

As they made the Land Rover climb up the hill towards the castle, Bobby noticed something she had never noticed before.

"Xander… "

"Mmm?"

"How long has there been a flag flying on the castle?"

"There hasn't, the flag only flies when there is a Balfour in residence, which will be, I suppose, when I eventually move in. Why?" He said this without taking his eyes of the road ahead.

"Because unless my eyes are playing tricks on me, there is a flag flying from the tower on the castle."

Alexander suddenly and without warning swerved the Land Rover into the side of the road to a grinding halt, before looking up to the top of the hill where Balfour Castle stood proudly, and there for all to see was a flag fluttering in the breeze.

"What the…what on earth…"

Alexander drove the Land Rover out from the rough turf on the edge of the road and drove off a little recklessly in the direction of the castle. Turning through the large ornate metal gates, and on to the

gravel path. As the Land Rover
sped up the drive spitting gravel out
in all directions, directly in front
could be seen the two little figures
of Rory and Mari and the faithful
dogs which had waited patiently for
Alexander's return.

Rory and Mari instantly sprang to
their feet on spotting the Land
Rover came hurtling towards both
Alexander and Bobby.
 As they emerged from the abruptly
halted vehicle the children each
took a hand.

"You have to come with us,
Mummy and Daddy said we had to
bring you as soon as you arrived,
hurry, hurry you're going to love it,

it's a big surprise," Said Rory, almost giving the game away, until Mari warned him to stop. "Shush Rory, remember it's a surprise," Mari said holding her free finger up to her lips in a gesture of secrecy.

As the children excitedly led both Alexander and Bobby up the stairs into what Bobby was to find out later was Alexander's father's old bedroom, to find Morag and Duncan, hurriedly putting the final touches to a completed double bedroom. With a large luxurious double bed in the centre of a huge oak panelled wall, and on either side stood two beautiful Japanese lacquered cabinets, on which sat two huge table lamps giving the room a beautiful soft glow. There were eastern rugs on the floor on either side of the bed and beautiful chaise longue at the base of the bed upholstered in the most delicious cream brocade.

A massive fire place was already laid as if ready for a chilly evening, with two beautiful ornate chairs set on either side. And on a small occasional table laid between the two chairs was a tray on which stood a bottle of red wine and two beautifully carved stemmed wine glasses.

"Surprise!" Yelled all four members of Alexander's slightly out of breath family, Morag's face was slightly pink from the exertion of preparing the room and Duncan

also looked slightly worse from the
sheer exhaustion no doubt of
pulling the enormous bed into the
room.

"What on earth?"

"We've moved you in!! Well you
wouldn't have done it, you would
have kept finding excuses until you
had completed every square inch of
the place. And… well… you
couldn't expect Bobby to live in
that outbuilding, and you couldn't
live in the shack… so as soon as
you told us Bobby was coming
back with you, and then we knew…
we knew it would be good news…
it is isn't it? Good news?"

"How on earth? How the Hell did you know that… and yes it is good news..."

Alexander stopped, long enough to fold his arm around Bobby's shoulder in order to make his announcement which the waiting group were sure he was gong to make.

"Bobby and I are engaged to be married."

A triumphant "Yess!!" Was shouted by all four, especially Morag.

"How wonderful, congratulations to you both, I couldn't be more pleased… and, less surprised… you didn't think we would go to all this trouble if we didn't think it was inevitable did you?"

The assembled group all laughed at amazement at Morag's confidence in her women's intuition, Duncan stated, it had nothing to do with him, but he was glad he hadn't lugged that massive bed in there for no reason, that was for sure. After the congratulations and hugs and kisses were over Morag pulled Duncan's arm discreetly and ushered both children out of the room so that Alexander and Bobby could familiarise themselves with their new bedroom.

Bobby's cheeks were slightly pink at the thought that both Morag and

Duncan had prepared a bed for them but Alexander explained that Duncan and Morag were very unconventional even though they appeared to be an old married couple they had their own little secrets. And besides, he told Bobby, "They are just a wonderful family, the best a guy could have, all they have ever wanted was my happiness.

"They've put up with a lot since I was injured; they spent every minute they could travelling all the way down to Birmingham without a word of complaint.

"And then you arrived, and turned everyone's life upside down, not only loving me but helping me to emerge from such a dark place, means everything not only to me but to them too. I wouldn't have dared come back without you, they told me exactly what they thought of you, how wonderful, indispensable, beautiful, caring, all of which I already knew, when I chased you back to your station knowing what I must do.

"So I'm not surprised they went ahead and prepared our… Marriage…bed…it's because they care about us both, so don't be embarrassed not with Duncan and Morag, and never with me."

It was then that Alexander suddenly remembered something and hurried to the door, shouting down the stairs to Duncan.

"Hey, how the hell did you get the flag up their on your own, you maniac?"

"With great difficulty little brother, but you're worth it," Duncan called up the staircase to his brother's jovial banter.

"Now there is a Balfour in residence once again, the flag must fly again."

The End

Epilogue

The nights that followed in the grand master bedroom were full of love and passion, and the days were full of last minute preparation for all three businesses but most of all, the evenings spent sitting around Morag and Duncan's kitchen table were very special indeed.

The wine and conversation flowed until all parties could hardly keep their eyes open, and laughter such as Duncan and Morag had never heard in the gatehouse for a very long time and which made them both feel happier than they could ever have imagined less than a year ago.

Bobby decided to ring Penny and Suze and suggest if they would like to come up on Friday morning two extra pair of hands would be very welcome if they could get cover for their own businesses. It was clear by both girls answer that nothing except a natural disaster would stop them from coming for the grand opening on Saturday morning.

As Alexander and Bobby strolled back from the gatehouse on their last night alone together in the castle, Alexander's hand was casually slipped into the rear waistband of Bobby's jeans, her hand was possessively around his waist underneath his t-shirt, as though they couldn't bear to be separated even for a moment.

Even Tariq and Nazim it seemed had accepted that their master now spent more time with Bobby and even they were fine with the new pecking order.

After a night of tender slow lovemaking, they showered together before emerging to start the day which promised to be frantic but exciting. During a very noisy and enthusiastic planning over breakfast at Morag's, it seemed everyone had last minute jobs, each more important than the other until Duncan spotted the battered old Citroen of Bobby's pulling up into the forecourt and out jumped Suze and Penny. Their jaws were aghast in awe and splendour of the castle, which Bobby was almost ashamed to say she had begun to take for granted and never thought about it being so grand anymore. To her and the rest of the family it represented a lot of money and hard work to simply make it habitable, and to finish the rather empty interior they needed for the businesses to be as successful as Penny and Suze's were becoming.

The whole family emerged from the kitchen and Bobby ran to hug both of her friends as they gasped and gaped at the sheer magnificence of the castle. Alexander introduced the girls to Duncan and Morag and the children and even Tariq and Nazim who he said were soft as lambs so there was no need to be nervous.

"My God Bobby, when you said a castle, I never thought… well, you don't do you… I mean a castle and it's even got a flag and everything."

"Ha, ha, that's exactly how I reacted, however Alexander and Duncan soon put me right, apparently in the winter its freezing and at present the whole idea of starting all the little ventures is to make enough money to be able to put central heating in for the coming winter. But you're right, it is very grand and I'll never get used to living in a castle no matter how long I live here."

"Hey, what do you mean how long you live here, there is no escape from this castle, we even have our

very own dungeon, don't we kids,
so watch yourself."

Morag and Duncan were dying to
show off their own creations, the
market garden Duncan explained to
the girls has all fresh produce and
it's sustainable for most of the year
and in the winter we will sell winter
vegetables and fresh and bottled
produce. The whole shop had the
kind of smell that reminds you of a
harvest festival, making the produce
irresistible.

The tearooms which were Morag's
domain, were so warm and cosy,
and gaily painted with their
gingham table clothes and pine
furniture. She had also bought the

second hand chilled display cabinets which Suze had suggested, for the cakes and scones and after Morag had given them an extra clean they looked almost new.

The gift shop was all decked out in a selection of Balfour Tartan items, such as t shirts, tea towels, mugs, place mats, et cetera you name, it they had bought it after finding a perfect site on the internet who after a fair amount of haggling on Bobby's part gave a decent discount for bulk and future orders [they all hoped].

"The only fly in the ointment is until we see how things go we can't afford to employ any staff. So tomorrow for the grand opening

Penny and Suze, we need your help. If it all takes off then we would probably advertise in the village for a couple of women, one for the gift shop and one for the market garden produce.

The tearooms are Morag's baby, but I'm sure Morag would love you to help her tomorrow wouldn't you?"

"Can I make a suggestion Morag? Have you thought about making some trays up with bite size tasters like they do in supermarkets just to entice customers in? Just for the grand opening of course, you don't give your produce away normally."

"That's a wonderful idea Suze; we could make them today if you're game?"

"Lead me to the oven; it's where I work best!"

"That leaves you Penny, what suggestions do you have for the gift shop? Just to entice people in?"

"Well I think first of all I would like to put some sandwich boards outside advertising the fact that it's the gift shop. What do you think?"

"Well actually Rory and Mari are excellent at making posters, how about they do the painting of the signs and Duncan could you make …say about ten or twelve wooden stakes with a sort of flat piece to pin the advertisement to then they could be pushed into the ground from the gates leading to the gift shop."

"No problem madam, you can see what she will be like Penny once she becomes the Laird's wife… we'll be touching our forelocks before we are allowed to speak."

"You aren't a Laird are you Alexander…?" Bobby said with a gasp of horror.

"Well strictly speaking the elder son is the Laird, although it is usually whoever lives in the castle; however the title has never been used for over a century so you don't have to worry, unless of course you want the commoners to doff their tatty cap at you?"

It was late in the afternoon before everything it would seem was completed and the decision was made to finally stop. It was then that Morag suggested they all had a BBQ on the beach as both Suze and she had done enough baking for the day and it would be nice if the men did the cooking for a change.

It was still very hot, even though it was early evening and they all hoped that the weather would hold for the grand opening the following day. The weather forecast had been checked and there were no apparent surprises in store, so this evening was all about, good food, good company, and relaxing.

The breeze from the sea helped to cool them off after the stresses of the day. The smell of food cooking on the BBQ was wonderful, and Suze and Penny collapsed onto the rug which Bobby and Alexander had brought out of the cottage as well as the usual pile of cushions. As they all relaxed for the first time that day, telling each other that if every day was as exhausting as that they would never stand the course.

It was then that Suze and Penny noticed the shack on the beach for the first time.

"Is that the cottage, the cottage you hired, right here on this lovely beach, with the ocean right on your door step?"

"Cottage, ha, ha, cottage," This Duncan was saying in a derisory tone.

"That I may add is our beach shack, we used to stay in that all night when we were kids didn't we Xander? Bobby named it a cottage," he said to Suze and Penny.

"Don't embarrass me, I feel bad enough about it, I advertised it thinking only that a fisherman would hire it, I never dreamed a woman would hire it… a woman called Bobby who I still thought was a man when I received her deposit… I nearly died when I spoke to her and realised she was not only a woman but a rather lovely woman, and a novelist, staying in my shack."

"But it's wonderful, can we go and have a mooch around?"

"Of course you can but I don't understand? What is it with you town folk; do you all think tatty old shacks are country cottages?"

"You don't understand Xander I told you us peasants don't get to meet folk like you with their own private beach complete with beach hut, let alone a castle."

"Come on, I'll show you round."
Bobby offered.

The two visitors came back outside
the cottage saying they absolutely
loved it! And they would rather
stay in there than in the castle with
its bare floorboards and camp beds.
"No offence Alexander, or to you
Bobby, I knows it's all for one and
one for all, but you have a bed and a
mattress and a Prince Charming to
sleep with, where as we have camp
beds and sleeping bags."

"Just imagine, we can get out of bed
and straight into the sea for a dip
before we start our big day!"

Alexander and Duncan both rolled
their eyes saying, women,

indicating they would never understand them, but agreeing they were more than welcome to use the shack, and the linen had been changed by Morag since Bobby had used it.

"Hey don't think we wouldn't love to stay in the castle with you, but we think we'll invite ourselves back once you have beds in the rooms and more than one bathroom, if you don't mind?"

As the night came to a perfect close everyone wanting to have an early night in preparation for the big day ahead. The party broke up when the fire on the beach was no more than embers as everyone said their goodnights.

. . . .

The Grand Opening

The grand opening was as great a success as it could have been, no one could have predicted that a simple ad in the local press, and posters placed in the shop windows in town could produce the multitude of visitors, even before the official opening time of 10am in the morning. Which was thought to be a very reasonable time for shoppers, however by 10am the designated car park was almost full and it was very obvious that a much larger car park would be required in future.

The tearoom was full to capacity until it closed at 4pm with all but a few scones and cakes left, and as many leaflets were taken to ensure a return with various ladies' groups, Morag was told. Duncan's fresh produce made such an impression on the locals; he was asked if regular orders for fresh vegetables could be placed. And the gift shop did a roaring trade selling the most obscure items that Bobby had insisted on buying such as baseball caps with the Balfour flag crest on, t-shirts went down a treat as did the smaller children's soft toys of all things, which Rory and Mari had suggested.

It was obvious that not only were the new ventures going to be a great success, but Morag couldn't have been happier than she was in her own little tea room and it was obvious that Duncan took great pride in showing off his home grown produce. So who was to say that he may in the future join Morag in having a change in career if all continued to do as well as they hoped.

Suze and Penny returned to their own individual creative ventures with even more zest than before, feeling the renewed excitement of Duncan and Morag's enthusiasm. They were both invited to return any time they wanted and were welcome in either the cottage or the castle… When the rooms were furnished of course.

But for the foreseeable future, Morag would enjoy her own little tea room, Duncan would continue to enjoy his garden, knowing now his produce was not only being appreciated but sold for profit. Alexander would continue his labour of love and restore the castle to its former glory and as for Bobby, she would write her Magnum Opus, but not for self gratification as she first thought, but to highlight the pain and suffering that war brings to all concerned no matter what colour creed or religion you were. And when her book was written it would be called.

To Hell and Back – A Soldier's Tale
By Roberta Lennox
In collaboration with
Major Alexander Balfour